ALL SHA IBERIBE

D0356793

NO LONGER PROPERTY OF
SEATTLE PUBLIC LIBRARY

KASIMMA

COPYRIGHT © 2021 Kasimma
All rights reserved.

DESIGN & LAYOUT Nikša Eršek
PUBLISHED BY Sandorf Passage
South Portland, Maine, United States
IMPRINT OF Sandorf
Severinska 30, Zagreb, Croatia
sandorfpassage.org
PRINTED BY Znanje, Zagreb

The following stories were first published
in various forms in the following publications:
"My 'Late' Grandfather," *Kikwetu Journal*;
"Jesus' Yard," *Jellyfish Review*; "This Man," *The Puritan*;
"Ogbanje," *The Book Smuggler's Den.*

Sandorf Passage books are available to the
trade through Independent Publishers Group:
ipgbook.com | (800) 888-4741.

National and University Library Zagreb
Control Number: 001103383

Library of Congress Control Number:
2021936945

ISBN: 978-9-53351-340-9

ALL SHADES OF IBERIBE

KASIMMA

SAN-
DORF
PAS-
SAGE

SOUTH PORTLAND | MAINE

DEDICATION

Maka ndi gara aga — to those who have gone.

Ọnwụ abụghị njedebe. Ọ bụ mbido.
For Uncle Ifeanyi Ezeanu na and others
who have gone before us.
Laaba nụ na ndokwa. Ọ ga-adiri ụnụ mma.

Trail of Tales

My "Late" Grandfather

A PIERCING SCREAM woke us all up. It was dark inside and out-side. I grabbed my flashlight, turned it on, and looked at the wall clock: 5:50 a.m. I heard loud stamping of feet as if people were running. My sister and I wore our jackets and rushed outside with the rest of the family into the wheezing and slapping cold of the harmattan. Everyone gathered outside, just in front of the house as if forming a barrier against the intruder. My sis-ter and I tried to get past them to see clearly, but a strong hand held our ears and dragged us back.

"Get inside!" our mother commanded.

We retreated, but we knew, even she knew, that we would not go inside.

"Don't look at him! Nobody should look at him!" somebody shouted.

I had no idea who said that. We were about fifty of us living in that massive compound. My grandfather had six sons and three daughters, thirty-five grandchildren, one brother—that we know of—five nephews, two nieces, thirty grandnephews and grandnieces. That is more than fifty, right?

"Jee kpọ Ezenwaka!" somebody screamed.

"Ezenwaka is coming," another replied.

I did not understand what was happening. Don't look at who? Why were they all raising their heads slyly to peek at the figure?

"What is going on?" I whispered to myself.

"Someone is sitting on Grandpa's grave."

"Cheta, is that you?" I asked.

"Yes," he whispered back and picked his nose.

I no longer doubted it was my cousin. He was always "digging" his nose. Sometimes, I prayed to God to help him find the gold he sought in there so that he could leave his nose alone.

"Did you say somebody is sitting on Grandfather's grave?"

"I did not say 'on.' I said, 'in front of.'"

"That's a lie. You said 'on,'" my ten-year-old sister, Ifeoma, countered.

"Who is the person?" I asked Cheta.

"Grandpa," he responded, boldly, implying that he knew exactly what he was saying.

"You mean Grandpa's ghost is on his grave? How did it come out of the grave?" I asked, suddenly drenched in sweat.

Cheta sighed and shook his head.

Ifeoma's sweaty, shaky, goose-pimpled body touched me. "Ije, please come with me. I want to ease myself."

"I cannot go anywhere o. Didn't you hear of the ghost? Urinate here, abeg. Nobody will beat you."

That was when I heard the husky voice of Ezenwaka, my octogenarian granduncle, singing incantations. He spoke Igbo, I am sure, but it sounded like Swahili, I guess. A white wool lappa was secured firmly around his waist, knotted under his navel. His fleshy torso, hands, face, and feet were decorated with nzu, the local white chalk used to purify oneself before approaching the gods. Slung on his right shoulder was a slim goatskin bag.

"But Grandpa was buried six months ago," I said.

"A branch of a palm tree was buried in his stead," Cheta answered matter-of-factly.

"One more word from any of you and I will send you to your room," my mother said between clenched teeth.

I promised myself not to utter another word. I did not want Grandpa's ghost to catch me on the way to my room and zap me away to the land of the dead. But what did he even come back to do? Then I recalled how Grandpa died. They said he drowned in Agwa River, where he had gone to wash his bicycle. Nobody saw him drown. There was no corpse. The only thing they brought back was his bicycle, his shirt, and the bathroom slippers he had worn out that day—which were found by the riverbank. Some even said he committed suicide and, as was the custom, he should not be buried. For lack of proof of suicide, Grandpa was given an expensive befitting burial. Now, after all the money spent and "compulsory cows" slaughtered to secure his soul a smooth passage to the land of the ancestors, he'd resurfaced.

Ezenwaka's voice distracted me. I heard other loud voices and stamping feet coming from the direction of the gate. I could not miss this history. I lay on the ground and peeped between everyone's legs. I saw Ezenwaka pick up a handful of sand and pour it on my grandfather's chest. Grandpa did not move, his gaze fixed on Ezenwaka. Ezenwaka did that three times before he brought out a kola nut from his bag, chewed it, and spat the contents on Grandpa. He drank from his green bottle of Aromatic Schnapps and spat some of it again on Grandpa. Grandpa stayed still. I began to wonder if Grandpa was even alive. Ezenwaka began another round of incantations.

Still singing, Ezenwaka slowly danced to the kitchen area. He came back carrying Grandma's biggest white fowl. Ezenwaka held the struggling, cackling bird by its legs and used its body to hit Grandpa several times. Ezenwaka hit Grandpa's back, front, rubbed the fowl on Grandpa's hands and legs, and hovered it thrice around Grandpa's head in a counterclockwise direction. Still holding the convulsing fowl on Grandpa's head, Ezenwaka dug his left hand in his bag and produced more kola nuts. He threw them on the ground, raised the fowl, and said in Igbo, "Ala, the goddess of fertility and the very earth, please accept these kola nuts we bring to you. God of our ancestors—" he reached into his bag again and produced some alligator pepper—"take this pepper to make the kola nuts tastier." He scattered the pepper on the ground, brought out some more, and threw them at Grandpa. "We ask you, Ala, the kind, to please release, from your sacred womb, the spirit of our brother, Ike, and take this fowl in his place, for we buried him in error."

He sang more incantations, dancing around the grave. He roared, to no one in particular, "Quickly! Come and dig a fresh grave."

The young men scurried away, giving me more room. I jumped up and filled in one of the blank spaces. My twelve-year-old body was slim enough to slide into the front and short enough to be hidden from the view of my mother.

I watched Ezenwaka sing and dance gracefully as he rained praises on Ala. The men dug frantically. While some dug up the grave behind Grandpa, others dug a new grave beside the old one. When they finished, some of them rushed off and returned with a palm tree branch.

"Ala, the kind, please accept the blood of this fowl," Ezenwaka said, squeezing the neck of the chicken until it detached from its body while he held on tighter to its dying body. He poured some of the blood dripping from the neck of the beheaded bird on the ground where the kola nut lay and some on Grandpa's head. "Let it cleanse Ike from the filth of the grave and also open the gate to the land of the living for him."

Finally, Ezenwaka threw the body of the bird in the new grave.

"For what you have eaten, Ala, the kind, you cannot vomit. Therefore, take this log in replacement of the one we buried in place of Ike's body. Ala, the kind, please accept these and release Ike's spirit back to us."

He instructed the men standing by the graves to exhume the old log from the old grave and throw the new log into the new grave with the fowl. When they were done, he asked them to toss the old log and cover both graves.

We all watched in silence as the men worked. As soon as they finished, Ezenwaka smiled at Grandpa as if he was seeing him for the first time, helped him up, and embraced him lovingly. Everyone rushed forward to embrace Grandpa. I stood there wondering why they ran away from him the first time and why it took all that show for them to embrace him.

I knew we were in for a long story of where Grandpa had been for close to nine months. I grabbed Ifeoma's hand, and we rushed to the bathroom to ease ourselves, then come settle down with the others to listen to Grandpa's story.

Jesus' Yard

SO, BORED TO death by my parents, brother, and God-knows-how-many servants in our "mansion" in Abuja, I decided to go and visit my aunt who lives in Jos. Aunty Nkiru is not a sibling to one of my parents. She is the granddaughter of my mother's step-great-grandmother's father's seventh wife. Wow! I cannot explain how Aunty Nkiru and my mother are still in touch after so many watered-down generations. I just know—evident from the pictures—that whenever my mother put to birth, Aunty Nkiru always came for omugwo, the traditional "child visit," because my mother—the last of five children and the only one living in Nigeria—is an orphan, and my father's parents live abroad.

I insisted on taking the public bus instead of allowing one of our drivers to cruise me to Jos. Aunty Nkiru, I was assured, would be at the park waiting for me when I arrived. I was still struggling to pick her out from the horde of bodies crawling like ants on sugar when I heard someone scream my name and wave. I did not see her face, but I recognized her voice and saw her flabby hands swaying like a flag in the wind.

"Chinelo!"

There was buxom Aunty Nkiru running toward me, flapping everything on her body apart from the features of her face. When she embraced me, her entire body—and I mean this literally—enveloped me the way an envelope protects a letter. I inhaled the stench of sweat that oozed from her sweaty neck and soaked clothes. Hands clutching my shoulders, she scrutinized me—like one would do to a favorite cloth before hanging it out to dry—and sucked me back into another hug, swaying from left to right. I was indeed happy to see her again after over a decade. She looked older but as beautiful as ever. She still had that unique smile that made her eyes lie down, just as I remembered it.

"Nelo, nwam, I know it is only you who will remember me. Nnọọ."

She reached to help me carry my big box, but I stubbornly declined. She shrugged, held my hand, and dragged me along.

"See how bony your hand is," she said in Igbo. "It is quite ironic how you rich people look so hungry and we poor people look well-fed. Anyway, how won't you look so hungry! After all, when you rich people see food, you touch it the way chickens pick their grains and say you are filled up. We, we don't play with food. When we see food, we eat to our fill."

I hungered for the fresh egg rolls I saw for sale on a tray. A hawker selling bottled water passed by. I wanted to buy some, but Aunty Nkiru walked very fast.

"Do you even understand Igbo?" she asked, loudly, in Igbo.

"Yes, Aunty," I replied in English.

"Do you speak?"

"Yes, Aunty."

She became distracted when we reached the park's gate—which I assumed was perpetually open because rust had eaten off more than half of the gate from below. I made the mistake of asking Aunty Nkiru for her car.

"Did you buy one for me?" she teased and nudged my shoulder before flagging down a motorcyclist. His jeans had a little tear by the knee. "We are going to enter this okada. Have you entered okada before?"

"Yes, Aunty."

She looked at me and smirked. I did not need my guardian spirit to tell me that she had seen through my lie. What were my father's numerous cars doing there that I should get across town on a motorcycle?

"So, we will share one to save money."

"We will what? You must be joking, Aunty." I started laughing.

"Be there laughing like a lizard. Climb and shift for me," she said, putting my box in front of the motorcyclist.

"Aunty, mba. There is just no way I am getting on that thing with you. Three of us on this! Plus, this big box! Are you kidding me?"

"Bịa, Chinelo, don't waste my time. Three of my size can fit on this bike comfortably."

"Three of who!" I couldn't stop laughing. Aunty Nkriu was always sarcastic, one could no longer tell when she was serious or not. I flagged down another motorcyclist and mounted. I pointed to Aunty Nkiru's okada. "Follow them."

Jos was hot, windy, rowdy, and busy—at least most of the places we passed. The motorcyclist, who rightly assumed that I was a visitor, gave me a little tour. He pointed out the yellow Terminus Main Market. When we got to Lion Bank at the roundabout, I was blown away by the big black statue of a fat woman carrying a baby on her side and a basket on her head. She was posed like someone walking and her mouth was in the shape of "O" as if she was also talking. It was an incredible work of art! We passed so many shops, especially on the busy but smooth road of Ahmadu Bello Way. I was vainly trying to pick out shop number 11 because that was where Aunty Nkiru's husband sold electricals: Rosebud Electricals. The road started becoming less busy after we passed St. Paul's Anglican Church and Jos Stadium, which was opposite Methodist High School. It became even more serene around Fatima Catholic Church, Fatima Private School, Paco Hospital, Chilas Hospital, and then into the heart of Apata. I saw two little girls of not more than seven years, strolling in the heat and holding the hands of their stark-naked baby brother. I was thinking about that when the motorcycle pulled to a stop.

"Nne, we are here," Aunty Nkiru announced.

I climbed off the bike. "How much," I asked her, opening my designer bag.

"Fifty, fifty naira each."

"Fifty naira from where?" the man who carried her barked. "Abeg, your money is one hundred naira per person."

"Onye oshi! You will come and vomit that hundred naira right here," Aunty Nkiru charged, arms akimbo. "If we remove everything you are wearing, it'll not amount to hundred naira. It is only if we remove your big head and join that we can get eighty naira. And it is the head without the brain o! Because there is nothing in the brain!"

I guffawed even if Aunty Nkiru looked and sounded serious.

"Look at you, bag of palm kernel," said the man in Igbo. "See how your weight made my tire flat." He turned off his motorcycle as if preparing for a fight.

"Is this one tire? Wretched man! Abacha!"

I was there wondering which "abacha" Aunty Nkiru meant? Abacha the general, or abacha the dried cassava salad?

He pointed at Aunty Nkiru, his fingers very close to her eyes. "If you call me Abacha again, Amadioha's dog will lick your eyes this afternoon!"

"Abacha," Aunty Nkiru repeated, stubbornly.

"Call me that name again, and I will . . ."

"What?" Aunty Nkiru had raised her voice. Necks started poking out from the windows in the surrounding houses and people trickled out of their bungalows.

"Aunty, it is okay. No need for all these, biko. I will pay."

I quickly brought out the money from my bag, but she pushed my hand down.

"It is like you don't know what to do with money, isn't it? You want to give it to this Abacha."

He slapped his motorcycle. "I have warned you this mad woman to stop calling me Abacha. Call me Devil I will agree, but call me Abacha again and both of us will put our legs in one trouser."

Everyone, except me of course, knew he was bluffing. He knew that he could not touch Aunty Nkiru in that neighborhood and go free.

"Drop that your bony hand! Quickly shift that your local-fowl-lap that is lost inside those trousers. Let me come and put my leg because I am sure there is room for me in that stadium you call trouser!"

The onlookers erupted in cheers, clapping. "One zero!"

I was terrified. I quickly handed the irate man two fifty naira notes and gave the same to the guy I'd ridden with—who seemed not to be Igbo-speaking because he was completely quiet throughout the angry exchange. The irked man pocketed his money, thanked me, and started his motorcycle. He snapped a finger at Aunty, shouted, "Your God has saved you," and rode away.

"At least I have been saved. You need saving! Anụ nchi!"

The onlookers cheered again. I did not even notice when the second motorcyclist left. I began to wonder what I had gotten myself into by coming to this place where fighting seemed encouraged, and even cheered. Where I lived in Abuja, one could not play loud music without being accused of "disturbing the peace."

Aunty Nkriu dragged me forward.

"Mama A-boy! Mama A-boy!" the children and adults hailed Aunty Nkiru.

She suddenly became cheerful. I could not believe the swift change in her mood. She waved her left hand at them. "Kedụ nụ? This is my daughter from the white man's land!"

I bent closer to her ear. "Aunty, Abuja."

"Shut up your mouth."

"She just came back from America so she said let her come and see her dear poor aunty! Isn't she a nice girl?" Aunty Nkiru screamed even louder.

They all shouted different praises at me. "She is o! She is so humble!"

"See, they now like you," she whispered. "Now wave, ọsịsọ, and better smile."

I obeyed. They all waved back. "Welcome, Americana!" Some even said they were coming to collect their own "American wonder."

We finally entered Aunty Nkiru's compound. The name "Jesus Yard" was written boldly with pink chalk above the dwarfish, wooden, entrance. I added an imaginary apostrophe. Jesus' Yard consisted of seven flats that formed a U shape, and it had a sandy courtyard in the middle. The houses were old and unpainted. The cemented walls flourished in mold. Most of the houses had netted spring doors to keep mosquitoes out.

Aunty Nkiru opened the door to her own flat and screamed, "Where are these children? Chukwuwuikem! Ukamaka!"

"Ma!" They came running to the door.

The girl, Ukamaka, wore a loose, formerly white but now faded and transparent flowery gown. Her orange underwear glowed through the dress. Her brother who was about her age wore only oversized blue boxer shorts.

"It's like something is wrong with the two of you! Didn't you hear me come in?"

They shook their heads. "Mba."

"If I slap you eeh! What were you doing? Watching TV, isn't it? Shift let me pass."

They looked at me as if they were just noticing me. They curtsied and bowed respectively. "Good afternoon, ma."

I smiled at them. "Kedụ nụ?"

Aunty Nkiru looked me down and chuckled. "Ngiri-Igbo."

She turned to her children, frowned, and yelled, "You cannot help her? Where are your manners? Take that box to the room, fast!"

They tried to lift the box but it was too heavy for them.

"They didn't go to school?" I asked.

"They are on midterm break. But even if they weren't, they should have been back from school by now," Aunty Nkiru replied, calmly. She turned to her children. "Zuzuru nu puọ n'ụzọ!"

They made way for us to walk past. I held the curtain up for them to drag my box inside while waiting for my eyes to adjust to the darkness. A yellow bulb was lit, but everywhere still seemed dark. I watched the children forcefully push my box into the room that was demarcated by a very dirty curtain. By now, my eyes had adapted to the dim light of the sitting room. I was faced with a room with faded blue walls covered with enlarged family pictures. There was a small TV, a VHS player, and a radio on a chipboard wooden TV cabinet. The funny thing about that cabinet was that the TV partition had two covers. I went nearer and pulled the covers together—the TV became completely shielded. An open padlock hung on the hasp. There was a soft covering, made of different colors of wool, placed on top of the TV. The rest of the cabinet had no covers but had heaps of VHS and tape cassettes piled in them. I ran my index finger through one cabinet and rubbed off the film of dust with my thumb. I studied the pictures on the wall. There were baby pictures of all Aunty Nkiru's seven children, wedding pictures, and graduation pictures. There was even a burial picture of Aunty Nkiru's father, I guess, because, in that particular picture, she was dressed in black, carrying a picture of an old man and, maybe, dancing. There were framed pictures clustered on a long chipboard shelf that was nailed above reach, which went around the walls of the sitting room. A calendar filled with drawings of Eddy Nawgu hung on the wall—as if the sitting room was not already picture-laden. In my house, not a single picture on any wall; my father detests that. We keep albums instead. At one end of Aunty Nkiru's sitting room was a medium-sized, wide, ash-wooden table with six matching chairs around it. I should have called it the dining table, but I doubt anyone ate there because it was stacked with dusty books, church bulletins, newspapers, even toilet paper.

Aunty Nkiru came out of the kitchen wiping her hands on her lappa. "You like my house, don't you?"

"It is beautiful."

"Shut up that your mouth. As if it is anything to be compared to your big house."

"It might not be as grand as my house, but it is modest and beautiful."

I caught the proud smile on her face. She sat opposite the TV cabinet on the green three-seater sofa, which matched the green carpet. There were also four green puffy chairs, two each at both sides of the TV cabinet, and brown side-stools beside each one. The ash-wooden stools matched with the center table. The sitting room looked very neat. It appeared the carpet was well-swept and the cemented ground well-mopped ahead of my visit.

"Just wondering, why did that man get so offended when you called him Abacha?"

Aunty Nkiru chuckled. "Do you like Abacha? Isn't his hand too tight in ruling us?"

I snorted. "My father is a Lieutenant General, serving Abacha's government."

"Ehen, that is why you will like Abacha. Since the beginning of this 1996 till now that the year is dying, I haven't bought myself common bathroom slippers."

She had plunged into sensitive waters, so I escaped that line of discussion and went into the kitchen. It seemed as though it had not been on the list of places to be cleaned. There were old pots, some with one handle, some without handles, one had one good handle and one dangling handle. But they all shared in common the pitch-black stains from over usage on the kerosene stove. There was a wooden cabinet hanging on the wall, looking as if it was painted as an afterthought with the leftover red wall paint. From the kitchen, I moved to the room where the children had carried my box. I met them seated on the bed. They smiled at me. I returned their smiles. The room was filled with clothes, but the bed was well-laid. My box stood in a corner, occupying so much space. The room had the same dirty, worn-out blue wall as the sitting room. There was a square patch lighter than the rest of the wall. I guessed something must have previously hung there. There was no wardrobe but large woven baskets, overflowing with clothes. I returned to the sitting room. There was one more room, the one Aunty Nkiru entered to change her clothes, which I assumed was her room so I did not enter there. I sat beside Aunty Nkiru.

"Are you done?"

I looked at her and smiled.

She held my hand. "Nwam, I am so happy to have you here. Who am I that a big person like you should come and visit me?"

"Aunty, stop it," I said and fondly tapped her shoulder. "Uncle went to the shop?"

"Yesso."

I'd spoken to him three days ago, when I rang, informing him of my intention to visit them. He had been very excited to hear from me.

In a flash, the power cut out.

"Down NEPA!"

The hilarious "down NEPA" chorus coming from the street sounded so loud and rehearsed as if someone conducted it. I was still laughing when the power was restored.

"Up NEPA!"

I burst into another bout of laughter. Aunty Nkiru looked at me, confusion smeared on her face.

When I stopped laughing, I filled the awkward silence by asking after her children. She chuckled proudly and shook her legs. "The first three, girls, are married. You can see their wedding pictures on the wall. Their two younger brothers are working in Kano and Zamfara, respectively. I don't know what they are waiting for to get married. These are the last two."

"Oh, that's great."

"Where are these children?"

They came running out.

Aunty Nkiru asked them in Igbo, pointing at me, "Do you know who she is?"

They shook their heads.

"Are they twins?" I asked.

"Yes," she said, smiling. "Ten years old."

"That's lovely."

Ukamaka bent her head and grinned shyly.

"Her name is Chinelo. She is your aunt. Have you heard me?"

"Yes, ma."

"Your job is to make her comfortable for the . . ." She turned to me. "How long are you staying again?"

"One week."

"One!" She raised an index finger. "One as in ofu?"

She returned her attention to her children. "Your job is to make her comfortable for the two weeks she will stay here."

I rolled my eyes.

"Now, what do you say to her?"

"Welcome, Aunty Chinelo."

"Chinelo is fine," I said.

"Maka gini? You want to spoil them?"

I shook my hands in my defense. "Aunty, I did not say they shouldn't call other people 'aunty.' I just said they should call me by my name. I do not like being called 'aunty.' It makes me feel old."

"Old gini?" She turned to her children. "Call her 'aunty.' "

"Aunty, biko," I insisted, "I'd rather be called Chinelo. They can call themselves 'aunty' and 'uncle' all they like."

This time, Aunty Nkiru laughed.

"You better arrange that TV cabinet, lock that place, and give the key to me. Pray that TV gets cold before your father comes back."

Ukamaka rushed to the cabinet, closed the TV protector, padlocked it, and handed the tiny key to her mother.

"Gbafuo unu!"

They scampered away.

"So what of all the others who live in this compound?"

My aunty looked at me and smiled lopsidedly. "You'll see."

* * *

I indeed saw. When Aunty tended to something in the kitchen, I stretched out and fell asleep on the sofa. Singing and clapping children woke me up:

Who will eat my bread and butter
Bread and butter
Bread and butter
Who will eat my bread and butter
My dear lady
Cheers
Bread or butter?
Bread
Cheers
Sandalili sandalili
I am a doctor in my country (country)
Some of you know me well
If you look me up and down
You will know that it's true

Those and several other songs permeated my sleep, leaving me with a nostalgic feeling. I even dreamed of playing those games with some children. I was forced to wake up. My eyes opened to the faces of the twins so close to mine that I screamed. They ran away. My aunty came running in.

"Ọgịnị?"

"I...I..." I caught their pleading faces from behind the room curtain. "I had a bad dream."

"It shall not come to pass in Jesus' name."

"Amen."

"Well, now that you are awake, come outside. I'd like you to meet the neighbors. They have all just returned from the fellowship we organize once a week. I should have gone, but for you."

I rubbed my eyes softly and followed her.

"Our white woman!" they all screamed, once I emerged from the house.

I looked back in search of the white woman. They surely weren't talking about me. I'm any color but white. I cannot even pass for fair. My skin is brown. Or did they refer to my ashy hazel eyes?

Someone pointed at me. "It is you we are talking about."

"I told them that you are based in America. Don't fall my hand," Aunty Nkiru whispered into my ear.

I looked at her startled.

"Mama A-boy, what did you tell her? She looks like she's seen a ghost."

"I told her that any visitor in this compound work as a night watchman for the first night."

They laughed. "Don't mind her. She is just teasing you!" They laughed again. Aunty Nkiru introduced me to fifteen women, told me their states of origin, and what they sold in the market. They were either Mama this or Mama that, Aunty this, Sister that. She told me how many children each one had; how many people lived in whose house; where they worked; she pointed out the one who had no child; she even introduced one and said, "She is living with a man she is not married to. I don't know why they cannot just get married." I expected the girl to be offended, but she found the comment amusing. I had forgotten all their names by the time Aunty was done with the introduction but I remember that they were all Igbos, all their husbands were traders in the Terminus Market, and the Sisters were all slimmer than the Mamas.

"Welcome o! What did you buy for us from America? I hope you are getting married soon o! Don't allow those oyibo men to be touching you for free," and so many other awkward things they said. I smiled politely and rushed inside.

I ate my dinner of rice and chicken that was prepared specially for me. Aunty Nkiru even warned me. "This is just to welcome you. By tomorrow, we return to our mgbaduga, fufu, swallow."

My uncle came back around nine p.m. I could hardly make out his face in the dim light of the kerosene lamp, but he was stocky. After our brief hug and exchange of pleasantries, he went straight to the TV box, unlocked it with the key Aunty Nkiru had placed on top of the cabinet, placed his hand on the top of the TV, nodded his head satisfactorily, and locked it again.

Before I woke up the next morning, my uncle had gone to work. The ache I felt on my back and sides was my body's way of protesting the weakness of the mattress on which I'd slept. I felt as if I had spent the night on hardwood, shivering the whole time in my green, silky nightgown. Thankfully, there were no mosquitoes. I retrieved my toothbrush from my handbag and went to the sitting room. I met Aunty Nkiru there seated with her legs stretched out and crossed on the center table. She tied a faded yellow lappa on her chest and beside her was her black soap dish. Her red sponge hung on her neck.

"Did you sleep well?"

"Good morning, Aunty."

"Good morning, Nwam."

She put her legs down from the table and counted her fingers, starting from the smallest. "One, what are the things you want to do this morning?"

"Like?"

"Like brush, defecate, bathe, what else? That's all, isn't it?"

"Yes."

"Good. So, I will give you toothpaste. You take a cup, fetch water from the drum in the kitchen, and brush outside. After that, you shall take a turn to defecate and then bathe."

I hugged myself. "Take a turn?"

She chuckled. "Are you cold?"

"This place is really cold."

"Indeed, Jos is on a high altitude. Why do you think the state is called Plateau? Then you chose to come during harmattan. But you should be used to it. You always go to America."

"How come you are just tying that lappa? Aren't you feeling cold?"

"Am I supposed to wear a cardigan to the bathroom? Besides, my flesh is my natural blanket." She winked at me. "Will you bathe with hot water or cold water?"

"Warm water. How can anyone bathe with cold water in this weather?"

"Speak for yourself o. I wash with cold water. But if you must wash with warm water, you will boil the water when there are two people before you in the queue. Anytime earlier and the water will be cold before it gets to your turn."

Was she kidding me?

She stood and carried her soap dish. "Ngwa, nje."

I obediently followed her outside. The bathroom and toilet were on the opposite side of the courtyard, directly opposite our door. We stood outside our door. The mighty wind that rushed at me almost threw me down, but Aunty Nkiru caught me.

"Ahn-ahn, Oyibo! Adakwana! Don't fall o!" Mama Somebody said.

"All these bony children! Na so ikuku hang one of them for tree one day. That wind for blow am commot if no be say one woman rush go carry am come down."

"Liar!" shouted another Mama.

That was when my eyes adjusted to the foggy weather and I realized that there were indeed two queues. Everyone tied their lappa or their towel on themselves. A few of them were still in the first stage of brushing, same as me.

"Oyibo, how was your night?" Mama Somebody asked me. She did not even seem interested in an answer because she tapped the person in front of her in the queue. "Bịa, what is Mama Nkechi still doing in that toilet? She wan born pikin?"

"Do we know if she needs help in delivering the shit or what."

"Mana chere nu, wait let me ask. Ọ fanyego ncha?"

Sister Somebody opened her palm. "She never shuk soap for inside her yansh o!"

"Aunty, what are they talking about? Insert soap in her butt? Why?"

She whispered, "Mama Nkechi is always constipated. So, she has to always mold soap into the shape and size of a finger, dip it in water, and insert it into her buttocks several times before she can defecate."

"Her buttocks?"

"Her anus nau. Don't you understand simple English? Kpachakwara anya gị o. Mind yourself," Aunty Nkiru snapped, pointing at me.

"You mean she inserts soap into her anus? Whatever happened to laxatives? Who even inserts the soap into her anus for her?"

Aunty Nkiru shook her head and hissed.

"Mama Nkechi, please if your stone is not yet ready to be free, allow me to go and shit my water. I will soon shit in this compound o!" another Mama, who had been pacing around, cried out.

"Please o! Mama Kelechi, don't shit here o! Don't even try it! Mama Nkechi! Come out of there!"

I whispered to Aunty Nkiru, "Is this the only toilet in the compound?"

She nodded.

"As in the only toilet? For how many of you?"

"Over thirty."

I froze.

Mama Nkechi soon emerged from the toilet, clutching her stomach.

"Have you given birth?" Mama Kelechi shouted.

"No! Since you have an ocean in your stomach, go. When you finish, I go."

Mama Kelechi ran inside the toilet, closing the rough wooden door.

"Mama Nkechi, you have used your turn o! After Mama Kelechi, I am next."

"You lie! I give am my turn. I go take her turn. After all, I never even shit. My can of water is still there."

"That is your problem. You have used your turn. You want my shit to go back?"

"Let it go! One of us will shit in this compound today."

The chatter made me forget the cold. Mama Kelechi soon came out, obviously relieved, holding one big, rusted, tin.

An impatient Sister shouted, "Next! Next! Don't waste time please."

The next in line collected the tin, fetched water from the black metal drum close to the toilet, and disappeared behind the rough wooden door.

"What are they doing with the water?" I whispered.

"Flushing the toilet."

"That small container? To flush the toilet?"

Aunty Nkiru giggled. "When it is your turn to poo, you will understand."

The woman who'd just entered the toilet rushed out. "I cannot endure that smell. Nne Kelechi, is it only shit that you shit there?"

"Look, Mama Ikenna, if you don't want to shit, get out from that place. Where do you think you entered? Is it rice and stew you want to perceive before?"

"Oho! Don't mind her. Please shit your own and give chance there."

"Bịa, Mama Nkechi, go back and put that soap in your yansh then run around this compound as if you are a chasing fowl. That Aso rock will fall out of your stomach afterward. You'll see."

They laughed.

"This one I have not heard Mama A-boy's voice this morning."

"Eeh, she is talking to America. We are now old school. America will soon go. Soldier go, soldier come, barrack go remain."

Aunty Nkiru did not even act as if they were talking about her.

Aunty Nkiru and I were the last in the queue. I was in the toilet while she was in the bathroom. It was a cemented pit toilet, surprisingly very neat. When I finished excreting, I poured the tin of water on it, and everything flushed down. I could not believe my eyes. When I emerged from the bathroom, I saw that the children had formed their queue outside. It seemed they had been waiting for the adults to round off.

As the day progressed, one by one, the inhabitants of Jesus' Yard came in to see me. Each of them left with one of my belongings: shoes, necklaces, clothes — anything. I blamed Aunty Nkiru for that. My mother had asked me to give her three ankara fabrics. She raised her voice in adulation, ran into the compound, and began dancing. That was what attracted the neighbors and made them ask me for something too. Much to Aunty Nkiru's chagrin, I gave everyone something.

"You will have an empty box by the time you go back," warned Aunty Nkiru.

"Why do you think I came with a big box, Aunty?"

Instinctively, I had packed stuff for a lot of people, though I did not expect the number of people that surfaced. For justice's sake, I had to start sharing my personal belongings. I did not even mind giving them my box. Suddenly, we heard the most depressing ululation coming from the courtyard. I was startled, but someone casually asked, "Have they started again?"

"Let's go and watch the film."

We all filed into the sandy courtyard. We were not alone. Others had come outside too. Right there, a man was beating his girlfriend—the unmarried lady who lived with her boyfriend. The residents merely stared and, sometimes, even cheered. I wanted to go and help, but Aunty Nkiru squeezed my hand and dragged me back.

"Aunty, he will kill her!"

"Let him kill her."

"Isimbe! Isimbe! Drag his penis and he will surrender!" Sister Someone shouted.

I whispered to Aunty. "Who is Isimbe?"

"The girl getting the beating. Didn't I tell you her name yesterday? Don't distract me o!"

I would have remembered such a name. Isimbe. It must be a nickname for no parent can name their child "tortoise head." Isimbe's scream made me pay attention again. Her boyfriend had given her another thunderous slap.

"He will kill her! Please, someone, help!"

Mama Someone scowled at me and snapped, "Are you not someone? Go and help nau."

I took her challenge, confident in my black belt in taekwondo. Before Aunty Nkiru could hold me back, I rushed to them and slapped the man on his shoulders. He turned, fuming like an angry lion.

"Only weak men beat women," I said, arms and body braced up for a fight, pendulum stepping like a boxer in the ring, beckoning him with one finger. "Fight me."

The compound fell as silent as a library.

"Mama A-boy, they will kill that girl o," the woman beside Aunty Nkiru whispered, but because everywhere was so silent, I heard. They seemed afraid for me. My aunty did not shake. She warned me, didn't she? The man turned back to Isimbe, gave her another deafening slap that knocked her to the ground, and then faced me. He threw the first punch and missed. He also missed with the second and third. I punched him in the face twice, four times in his stomach, then I spun and landed a kick on his neck. He dropped on the ground like a felled tree. I withdrew from the cretin and roared, "Abacha!"

The quiet compound exploded in cheers and claps. "Chinko! Chinko!"

"He is not even a man. It is only a tortoise that he can beat!" they mocked him.

I was still enjoying my victory when someone started pounding my back. I turned and saw Isimbe hitting me and crying.

"Did I beg you?" she shouted. "You want to kill him for me?"

I landed a dirty slap on her neck; my five fingers imprinted like they would on a foggy mirror. She fell on him.

"Ụvụrụazụ," I said, disgusted by her.

Everyone cheered even louder. "Americana, you have given her the perfect name! Fish brain!"

Some even went to congratulate Aunty Nkiru who could no longer maintain her nonchalant look.

I tried to imagine a tortoise head with a fish brain. It made me feel slightly sorry for Isimbe. I shrugged, gave the man a hand, and helped him up, frowned at him, daring him to try anything funny. But he did not.

"Peace, bro. I come in peace." I raised my hands and dusted them afterward. "But you see this girl," I said, pointing at Isimbe on the ground, "knock the living daylight out of her. She deserves it! Keep knocking her until her empty head enters her neck!"

"Bruce Lee! Lee-lee! Leeliana! Jacking Chang!" they all hailed different names at me.

I chuckled. *Jacking Chang*? If only he knew.

The man helped Isimbe up. They limped to their room and locked the door. Everyone tiptoed close to listen. I stood aside. The veins and bones on Aunty Nkiru's neck and face bulged out. Soon, I heard Isimbe screaming: "Harder! Harder, Emeka! Aaaah! Aaaah! I'm cumming, Emeka! Don't stop! Akwa orgazim lee!"

I was more than disgusted. I suddenly understood the anger on Aunty Nkiru's face. How could Isimbe behave in such a way where children lived for goodness sake?

Shit Faces

NNEMEKA DASHED OUT of her hut, ululating like someone possessed by a malign spirit. She ran very fast for a fifty-three-year-old. She ran from her house, through the village district, through the busy Eke market, where, howling like a spirit, she created quite a panic. Some people ran for cover. Others made imaginary circles around their heads and snapped their fingers as if to dodge whatever curse she'd uttered. A fat woman relieved herself of the basket of oranges on her head so that she could run faster. Some women, the ones with a kind heart, cried out to the young men to run after Nnemeka. Some teenage boys, those whose mothers were not close by, joined the hue and cry in pursuit after Nnemeka. None of them could catch her. Only one person came close: Mezie, the cheater. Mezie still did not catch her. He chased her to the evil forest where he dared go no further. When Mezie returned to the village, tired, panting, arms dragging, a horde of people lurked around under the mango tree waiting for news from him.

"Ọgịnị?" they asked in an assortment of vocal pitches. "Kedị ya?"

Mezie supported himself by placing one arm on his knee and the other on his chest. His face was very close to Mazi Okafor's long-bearded goat. The goat blared in his face making Mezie stagger.

"Where is she? Can't you talk!" a septuagenarian screamed at him.

"Nne . . . Nnemeka . . ."

Baa!

"Ehen! Ehen! Nnemeka what!" another irked woman screamed.

Baa!

"Nnemeka ran into the evil forest!"

"Ewoo," they shouted, uniformly placing their hands on their heads.

Baa! Baa!

The quick-tempered Dike scoffed at Mazi Okafor. "Shut up that goat that looks like you before I snap its neck."

Mazi Okafor squeezed his eyes. "May Amadioha strike you dead if you say one more word to me!"

Dike snorted. A wiry man unhung his water gourd from his waist and gave it to Mezie. Mezie could not be more grateful. He gulped it all down, looking up, squinting into the sun's rays.

Baa!

Okoye, a scruffy young man in his thirties, bit his forefinger and flapped his palm. "We should report this news to the king. The king should have banished that thing from this land a long time ago."

"Yes!" they all agreed.

"Of what use is it . . ."

Baa! Baa!

"Of what use is it banishing her? Did you not hear him?" Nwoko, of about the same age, tall and lanky, responded, pointing at

Mezie. "She ran into the evil forest, the land of the spirits from where no mortal has ever returned. She is never coming back!"

"Yes!" they all chorused again.

Nwoko cut a handful of leaves and gave them to Mazi Okafor who stuffed them into his "twin's" mouth.

"It is not the first time she is running into that evil forest," countered Mgbeke, the fat woman who'd littered the market with her oranges.

"Yes!"

"But how do we know?" argued Ada, the beautiful newlywed, scratching the scar on her left eyebrow. "It is only rumors!"

"No!"

"How do you know she does not go there? Or do you go to the evil forest as well?" Mgbeke refuted Ada.

"We should report her to the king anyway," said someone.

"Yes!" they all agreed and dispersed, murmuring to one another as they headed to the king's residence.

* * *

The king and his chiefs sat in the royal *obi* enjoying a gourd of fresh palm wine. They heard the approaching crowd. The chiefs looked at each other as if to decode the reason for the unexpected visit on each other's faces. Two young men with strong fat arms and thighs, holding spears, stopped the villagers. Like the other young men of the village, they too tied only a small cloth, in the shape of a diaper, around their waists. One of them looked back at the king who signaled to let the villagers through. The guards uncrossed their spears and the villagers filed in. They stopped at the entrance of the king's thatched-roof bamboo hut and prostrated themselves, crying, "Igwe!"

"Bilie nu!" the king replied, raising his staff. "It is well with you all. Welcome."

They got up and dusted off their knees and hands. Without waiting for a prompt to speak, one of the young men in front exploded. "Igwe, we have come to report Nnemeka, the osu. Igwe, we are tired of Nnemeka in this village!"

"Yes!"

The king and his six chiefs waited for the noise to completely stop.

"What has Nnemeka done this time?" the king asked.

One of them told the tale that merited their visit. The king listened, rubbing his bearded jaw. It was not the first time that the villagers had reported Nnemeka and her bizarre habits, but he was not one to heed to the word of disgruntled villagers without first hearing both sides of a story.

*   *   *

The first time the king set his eyes on Nnemeka was when Nwoye came crying to him, carrying her daughter. She reported that Nnemeka beat up the six-year-old girl. The king ordered his guard to fetch him Nnemeka. When his guard arrived with her, he pushed her so furiously that she fell face down on the mat at the king's feet. The king shifted his legs to avoid contact with her skin. The guard bowed and dashed off, rubbing his palms together as if trying to scrub away something unwanted. Nnemeka raised herself off the ground like a snake and knelt before the king. He'd forever be grateful to his chi for giving him dignity enough, or something close to it, to restrain himself from covering his eyes when he saw her face. Nnemeka was so ugly; her skin was wan and white, like the belly of a snake. There were pink patches on her chest that resembled sunburn. A mess of freckles covered her face. She looked half-blind when she squinted her tiny, sleepy eyes to look at him. Her hair was as golden-yellow and as silky as corn silk. Her teeth looked as if she used a paintbrush to apply palm oil on them. She was as thin as his staff. Her breasts were as tiny as tangerines. He made a conscious effort not to look toward her crotch. But his curiosity got the best of him. He slouched when he did not see any man bulge. Was it then a mere rumor, he thought. He had never seen any living being—human, plant, or animal—as ugly as Nnemeka. The only positive thing that could be said about her appearance was that she looked at least twenty years younger than her age.

"Yes, Your Highness!" Nwoye cried out. "She is the witch that beat up my child!"

The king raised an arm. Nwoye kept quiet.

"Young lady."

"Your Majesty."

The king could not believe the nightingale voice that emerged from such ugliness.

"What is your name?" he asked, as if he didn't already know.

She looked down and murmured, "Nnemeka, Your Majesty."

"Look at me when I talk to you!" he roared, even if he was not sure he was strong enough to choke back his revulsion.

Nnemeka raised her head and bent it to the left. She exposed one part of her yellow teeth and squinted. Goosebumps ran down the king's back. He swallowed. Because he was a king, and could neither display fear nor weakness, he had to stare right back.

"Did you beat this little girl?"

"No, Your Majesty."

"Fib!" cried Nwoye.

The king frowned at Nwoye. "Speak one more time when not spoken to and I will have you whipped seven times on your breasts."

Nwoye shuddered and held her lips. The king nodded in satisfaction. He beckoned to the terrified little girl seated beside her mother.

"Nwam, bịa."

The girl sat still, shaking. Her mother nudged her. The little girl wobbled to the king. When she got to him, he lifted her onto his lap and held her trembling hands.

"Don't be afraid of me, ịnugo? I am your friend."

She nodded and smiled closed-lip. The king gestured to Nnemeka to put her head down. She obeyed and exhaled.

"My child, tell me the truth." He pointed at Nnemeka. "Did she beat you?"

The little girl stole a look at her mother, Nnemeka, and the king.

"Tell me what happened," the king whispered.

The girl timidly told a story of how, while at the farm, she wandered away, chasing a bird. She found herself in front of Nnemeka's compound. She saw Nnemeka crouched, digging the dry soil. She became transfixed by the sight. Nnemeka packed hot sand on her hands and threw it at the girl's chest. It was the burning heat of the sand that made her scream, drawing her mother to the scene.

"Nnemeka, is that true?" the king asked.

"Yes, Your Majesty."

The king sighed. For the first time, in the fifty-six years of his life and twenty-nine years of kingship, he felt unsure. He could feel Nnemeka's despondency, even if she posed as confident. Why did Nwoye not teach her daughter that staring was not only rude but foolish? But then who would blame the little girl for staring at someone as ugly as Nnemeka? Yet, Nnemeka should have had some compassion for the little girl and not thrown hot sand on her soft bare chest. Should he punish Nnemeka? That was justice. Or should he scold the little girl for staring? That too was justice. In the end, he apologized to Nwoye and her daughter on behalf of Nnemeka and sent them on their way. Nwoye thanked him from her heart.

"Next time, Nnemeka, be compassionate."

"Yes, Your Majesty."

She remained kneeling, and he was not prepared to ask her to stand. He whispered something to the guard beside him who bowed and ran off. The king asked her questions whose answers he already knew, attempting to take a peek into her brain.

"Where do you live?"

"At the outskirts of the village."

"And your parents?"

"Dead."

He shivered at her curt response. Was that what caused her sorry state?

"Have you any siblings?"

She had not raised her head since he'd asked her to put it down. "I'm an only child."

"Friends?"

"A bụm osu."

"Surely you must have friends amongst your fellow outcasts."

"No friends."

Sensing Nnemeka as mysterious, he sent her on her way. All that night, he thought about the outcast system. He had long considered abolishing it, but his chiefs would not approve. It did not make sense to him that slaves could mix with and even marry the freeborn, but outcasts could not. To him, outcasts were to be revered, not treated as lepers. Once, as a young man, learning kingship from his father, he raised the issue. He did not miss the sad look on his father's face when he explained. "An outcast," his father said, "is a freeborn who was dedicated to a particular god for its protection. People are afraid of these gods. Should you offend the wards of these gods, the gods will strike you dead at once."

The next day, at dusk, the king sent for two of his good friends, who were also his chiefs and members of his cabinet: Obi and Uchendụ. He allowed Uchendụ, the doyen, to officiate the ritual of breaking the kola nut. They bowed their heads while Uchendụ prayed over the kola nut, prayed over their kingdom and their lives. When he finished, he broke the kola nut into three, picked a lobe, and served his friends the rest. Each of them broke a bit of their share and threw it on the sand for their ancestors.

"Ndị enyịm, I have called you here to discuss someone of new interest."

Their faces immediately lighted up in impish grins. While the king narrated the previous day's encounter with Nnemeka, the grins on their faces faded.

Obi scratched his bald head. "Igwe, that girl is pugnacious."

The king bit his kola nut. "Is that her fault?"

"But, Igwe, she is osu!" Uchendụ snapped his fingers as if he was afraid of the word.

"I know she is osu. She even told me so."

"Osu to Ekwensu!" Uchendụ shuddered and spat on the sand. The fowls rushed, fighting for who would get the lion's share of the spit.

The king shook his head the way an animal would shake off water from its fur. He recalled what his father taught him about Ekwensu, the trickster god. His father had joked that when Ekwensu greeted you good morning, don't take its word for it.

Go and check the position of the sun because it must be afternoon. Ekwensu was the god of war, invoked by warriors—only at wartime and in the field of battle—never in peacetime. As a young man, the king experienced Ekwensu firsthand when he went to battle. They invoked it while hiding during a skirmish. Their enemies showed up, acting all confused and stupid. It was the easiest battle ever. So, the king reasoned that Ekwensu could trick its slave's provoker to death. No wonder nobody wanted to have anything to do with Nnemeka.

"It would have been better if she were a slave," Obi said, interrupting the king's thoughts.

Uchendụ filled his drinking horn. "Ohu na osu bụ ofu ihe." He drank up, ignoring the palm wine frothed on his moustache.

"No, I disagree. Slaves and outcasts are not the same," said Obi, struggling with the lappa hanging around his neck. "Slaves are better than outcasts. Slaves are also freeborn but they were captured at war. The only thing is that once a king dies, seven slaves must be buried alive with his corpse. How then are they the same as outcasts?"

Uchendụ belched. "And of all the gods, Ekwensu! She is an outcast amongst her fellow outcasts."

Though their arguments held the king spellbound, he felt even sorrier for the outcasts. "Why do we treat ndị osu like snakes?"

"But, Igwe, do you blame us? I can laugh with my friend here, Obi." He struck Obi's shoulder. "And strike his shoulder as I did and get away with it. Obi knows it is a joke. His chi knows that too, because Obi is freeborn. I can get away with teasing ohu and still be safe. The slave will do nothing. If I dare do the same to osu, I might fall and start foaming at the mouth. Igwe, if we do not isolate ndị osu, we will all die within two days!"

The king sighed and scratched the back of his left ear. If his conscience urged him to extend a hand of friendship to Nnemeka, he would. If her god chose to strike him dead, so be it. He said as much to his friends.

"Biko, Igwe, avoid that thing. Please, your heir is only twelve. Do you want to cross parts with Ekwensu? I can recommend a good girl in the village if you need a fourth wife," said Uchendụ.

The king exhaled and chuckled. He scratched his full, wooly, gray hair and picked his nose. As he rolled the mucus on his fingers, he said, "Something must kill a man. At least I've produced an heir and many spares. I do not want to marry Nnemeka. I am the king. I cannot marry osu. Nnemeka is my subject. I will extend a hand of reconciliation to her for all this village has put her through since her parents died."

"Parents? Dead? Is that what she told you?" Obi asked, arms akimbo, brows furrowed.

Uchendụ shook his legs. "She is an incorrigible liar as well!"

The king would not relent. He thought about Nnemeka all night. He could not imagine living in isolation like Nnemeka. If she could not trade even in the osu market, what then did she eat? Was that why she was so skinny? Why was her skin so white? Should he abolish this outcast madness? Would that even solve the problem?

He decided to visit her. The king asked his first son, Nwigwe, to go with him to Nnemeka's house. Nwigwe's mother rushed out and fell at the king's feet, begging him to leave her son alone. It took the timely intervention of his other wives to prevent the king from giving her a kick in the jaw. Her co-wives dragged her away.

Nnemeka's hut was thirty kilometers from the royal residence. The king and his son decided to walk, the guards holding a massive umbrella above their royal heads. The king enlightened his son as they strolled. "Nwam, you are going to be the king someday. I asked you to join me on this visit to teach you that you must see all human beings as equal. It does not matter if they are freeborn, slave, or outcast. That way, you can dispense justice without fear or favor."

"Yes, Father."

When they got to Nnemeka's house, they met two colorful curtains, two meters high, which served as her gate. The curtains hung from two sticks that hung on two big orange trees. The curtains ushered them into a large grassless compound. A hut stood to the right, opposite a mango tree. There was another hut a little distance away. One of the guards knocked on the wooden door of the first hut. Nnemeka opened the door as if she had been waiting for the knock, looking heavy-eyed.

She fell on her knees and bowed her head. "Your Majesty."

He did not pat her back. "It is well with you. Get up."

"Welcome to my home, Your Majesty. Let me get you a chair." She disappeared into her hut.

The king had to nudge his son who froze on seeing Nnemeka. "You are the son of a lion. Act like it!"

Nwigwe nodded.

Nnemeka came out with a bench that she placed in the shade in front of her hut. The king and his son sat, enduring the fetidness of her hut. She sat on the sand beside them and stretched out her legs. His guards stood under the sun.

"Let me get you kola nut." She sprang to her feet again, so full of life.

"Mba! Mba! Don't worry."

Nnemeka returned to her position, bent her head, and smirked. She picked a piece of nzu from under the bench. She drew three vertical lines on her foot, saying per line, "Eke, afọ, nkwọ." Then she drew the last horizontal line across the three vertical ones. "Oye." She opened her palms to the heavens, bowed her head, and prayed. "Chukwu okike, the god who has opened my eyes to see today."

The king and his son assumed the same praying posture.

"Ikukuamanaọnya, the god of my mother, the god of kindness. This day has come because you either willed or permitted it. I thank you for blessing an outcast like me with the visit of a king. May it be well with him."

"Ise!" the king and his son responded.

She prayed some more over the king, his household, and the village. When she finished, she squinted at the king and smiled. Her prayers moved him. He picked up the *nzu* from where she had dropped it and repeated the ritual of the four market days. He drew the horizontal line of *oye* first before drawing the vertical lines of *eke*, *afọ*, and *nkwọ* on top of *oye*. Afterward, he drew a line from his big toe to his ankle on both legs and passed the chalk to his son to do the same. By so doing, the king showed that he came in peace and demonstrated that he did not see her as persona non grata. Nnemeka looked at the king, chuckled, and lowered her head. In that brief moment, he saw her as a human being and not an ugly monster.

"Visits are alien to me. Forgive me if I don't attend to you well. You are the first person to ever visit me. You are welcome, once again, Your Majesty."

Looking at a fowl picking whatever from the sand, he said to Nnemeka, "Nnemeka, you are Nwogbokeke's daughter. Why did you lie to me?"

Nnemeka chuckled. "Forgive me, Your Majesty. Yes, indeed, Mazi Nwogbokeke is my mother's husband. But he has never been in my life as a father even though he is aware of my existence. That is why I assume that I have no father."

"But he cannot be in your life. He is freeborn. You are osu."

She shook her head. "My mother was born free and died free. She lived the life of an outcast because of me. Her husband could have sneaked in here once to see us or sent some of his harvest to us."

The king nodded, the corners of his mouth turned down. "I'd like to hear about that."

"Everyone in the village knows my story. Why do you think they avoid me?"

The king smiled, sighed, scratched his beard, and closed his eyes. After what seemed like five seconds, he opened his eyes. The smell coming from Nnemeka's hut and her body was malodorous. Unable to bear the smell, he announced that they move to sit under the mango tree opposite Nnemeka's hut. Nnemeka made to carry the bench but the guard halted her. When they settled under the mango tree, his guard fanning them, the king said, "You may speak now, Nnemeka."

Nnemeka proceeded to tell her story, drawing things on the ground when she pleased. She spoke with the ebullience of a storyteller.

"My mother, Ugomma, was her husband's first wife. She was childless. Her husband married two other women and produced sons and daughters. Though my mother had endured so much mockery on account of her childlessness, she did not give up on herself. She kept begging Ana, the goddess of fertility, to give her a child. She went from one shrine to another. She told me she ate and drank different concoctions. Once, she had to drink a bitch's breastmilk from the source.

"One day, my mother visited Ezeagwọ. This man, Ezeagwọ, was soaked in the knowledge of divination. His god, Idemili, made sure of that. He was in his nineties and lived in the mighty Ọgba cave, overseeing our Amawa village, and its environs. The most outlandish of all was that his cave slithered with all types, colors, and sizes of snakes. Maybe that was why nobody visited him. She found out that day that indeed, his name, Ezeagwọ, king of snakes, was not a joke. She froze at the irritating sight of those snakes. All she heard and saw were snakes until his voice echoed from inside the cave.

'Ugomma, daughter of Ozi, wife of Nwogbokeke, do not be afraid. Proceed.'

"She said she saw the scariest human being emerge from the mouth of the cave. He was very huge. His face looked like a giant tigerfish, but with small teeth. His white beard was as long as a horse's tail. His chest looked like a woman's, whose tired breasts had nourished many children. His stomach was big and looked strong as if there was a small pot inside. His body looked succulent as a woman's. His voice was coarse but at the same time sounded like a hiss. He held a staff full of bells, whose sounds had somehow escaped her. On his other hand was a lighted ogbodu, which served as his torch. My mother said she did not understand if she was looking at a man, woman, or spirit.

"She remained motionless. He smiled at her and beckoned her to come. According to her, the authority with which his hands moved gave strength to her legs. She moved like a zombie.

'Gaba n'iru. Don't be afraid.'

"My mother walked like a person possessed by a spirit, past all the slithering snakes, right to the mouth of the cave. He grabbed her hand with so much force that she jerked and felt the spirits flee from her. She had not noticed when he moved his fire-torch to the hand holding the staff. She looked around and saw herself surrounded by snakes. Before any sound could escape her opened mouth, he raised his hands.

'Don't shout here o. These snakes hate noise. For all they know, you are the one that came to their house.' He laughed aloud. 'If it is for these snakes, you have nothing to fear. But if you see a scorpion, get a stick and smash its head for I cannot

guarantee your safety. Why do you think I carry this fire about?'
He laughed again. 'Follow me.'

"She almost glued herself to him. His folded skin stank of stale palm kernel oil and sweat. His buttocks marched under his red cotton lappa like a buxom woman's rear. He led her to an average-sized room filled with carvings of his god. The walls leading to the entrance of the room slithered with snakes. It gave her the chills to realize that no snakes entered this room. She felt very safe surrounded by the gory carvings of gods. One was a bloody human skull. Another was the wooden carving of a short man sitting on a stool. It had the head of a cobra whose mouth was open and dripping with fresh blood. The next was a round face made of what she did not know. Its eyes were two cashew nuts and its mouth was a shell of groundnut. She said that at this point, she stopped taking in the details because she wanted to be able to sleep afterward.

'You want a child?' he asked.

'Yes, my father.'

"He beat his gong and sang incantations. He grabbed a gourd and tilted it over his opened mouth. A red liquid smelling like blood poured forth. He spat the liquid to his carvings and wiped his now red teeth with his tongue. Singing, he grabbed a handful of cowries from a calabash, shook them, and poured them on the ground. He looked at them, shuddered, packed them all up, and repeated the process. This time, he shook his head. His once vibrant eyes now looked thinned out.

'Nnaanyi, please what is it?'

'Nwam, it is better for you to remain childless.'

"My mother was so distressed. There had to be a way. She knew he was the only one to help her or she wouldn't come all the way. How then was he saying that to her?

"He repeated the process. This time, he sang louder and longer. When he rolled the cowries on the floor, he shook his head and reiterated the same message to my mother. My mother fell on her knees and began to cry. She told me that while she wept, he maintained an impassive face. After what seemed like an eternity, he tapped her back and asked her to sit. My mother obeyed. She cleaned her nose with her hand, smearing mucus on her lappa where she rubbed it off.

'If you heard me well, I suggested to you to stay childless. Not that you cannot have a child.'

"My mother's face lit up. She grinned.

'Nnaanyi, I am willing to do anything it takes.'

"He shook his head. 'Nwam, when a child eats the food that kept him awake, he goes to sleep. But should you eat this food, Ugomma, daughter of Ozi, wife of Nwogbokeke, you will never sleep. Go home. You are your husband's trophy. Everyone in the village knows you are the most beautiful. Isn't that enough?'

'No, Nnaanyi. It is not enough! They call me beautiful to my face and deride me behind it. A woman without a child is incomplete. I do not care about the darker days ahead. I will do anything to have a child. I have traveled for two days, through a lonely forest, with neither food nor water to come here. I cannot go back empty-handed.'

'Are you sure? Ugomma, daughter of Ozi, wife of Nwogbokeke, are you sure?'

'Yes, my father.' She struck her chest. 'I am sure.'

"He sang more incantations. Then he turned to her, wrinkled his nose, and puckered his lips.

'They asked me to tell you to state your need and affirm that you are ready for the catastrophe afterward.'

"My mother trembled. But because she wanted nothing else than to cradle her own baby, she turned to the carvings.

'I, Ugomma, daughter of Ozi, wife of Nwogbokeke, wish to bear a child. I will accept, without complaint, whatever future awaits me. There is nothing the eyes will see to make it shed blood.'

"He nodded, turned to his gods, and told them they have heard what she said. He sang incantations, his eyes glued to his carvings. He dug his hand into a clay pot wrapped in a white cloth. He brought out a kola nut, sang some more, broke it, ate half of it, and handed my mother the other half. She collected it and threw everything into her mouth.

'Nnọọ! The gods welcome you. They say you shall bear a child nine months from now.'

"My mother clasped her hands in joy.

'Take this.' He dropped something wrapped in a palm leaf on her hand. 'When you get home, put it in the food you will cook for your husband. When he eats it, he will lie with you, and you shall get pregnant. Ihe onye metere ya buru!'

"My mother grabbed the portion with both hands and tucked it in her cleavage. She did not mind his last warning that she should bear the consequences of her actions.

'I will perform some cleansing before you leave.'

"She nodded, grinning.

"He asked her to lie down, head up, hands beside her, legs straight, as a corpse lying-in-state. She obeyed. He sang songs, sprinkled some blood and water on her, danced around, and jumped over her thrice. He went to the entrance of the door and retrieved one of the small pythons. My mother moved back, but he shouted at her not to move. He held the python close to his lips and whispered to it. The thing raised its head.

'Open your legs!'

"My mother was aghast. 'Nnaanyi, ịsị gịnị?'

'You heard me. I said open your legs!'

"She immediately parted her legs.

'I will send this messenger into your stomach.'

'Chimo!'

'Keep quiet!'

"My mother managed to keep quiet, but she could not keep still.

'The stubborn ear gets cut off with the head. This is the least of what awaits you, Ugomma, daughter of Ozi, wife of Nwogbokeke. This snake will go into your womb and eat all the evil charms preventing you from conceiving. When it finishes, it'll crawl out of you and die, but you must lie still until it's finished. A toad that does not do its errand well will repeat it.'

"My mother tried to be brave. She did not want a repeat of the snake's cleansing. But as soon as the snake touched her skin, she fainted. She had a dream where the medicine man placed her on her bed. He ogled at her and bit his lower lip. He rubbed her cheek, his lips parting into a grin. Stepping away from her, he spun around and disappeared in a cloud of smoke. She woke up in her hut, coughing. She was naked, and her thighs vibrated. The hut smelled like a mixture of dust and water. She could not explain how and when she got there. All she had as an explanation was the dream.

"The next day was her turn to serve her husband dinner. She slaughtered one of her goats and made delicious onugbu soup. She did not forget to add the portion to his food. She took her time to look radiant before serving him in his hut.

"He tapped the bed. 'You are glowing tonight. You even made my favorite bitter leaf soup. What is going on?'

"She made sure her thighs touched his. 'Nothing. I am just happy.'

'How did your journey to Ezeagwọ go?'

'I did not go. It was too far. After walking for a whole day, I felt exhausted, and I knew I could not make it to that mountain alive. I decided to come back home and accept my fate.'

"He rubbed her back. 'Is it not what I have been telling you? Don't worry, ịnụgo?' "His hungry eyes feasted on her breasts.

'Thank you, my husband. I shall return for the bowls when you finish.'

"She smiled at him, licked her lips, and walked away. When she returned, he had finished eating. She bent down to pick up his plate, turning her rear to him, pushing it so close to his face that she heard him sniff. He asked her to close the door and windows. She turned to him and smiled. After locking the door, she left her lappa beside it and returned to him unclad. He squeezed her breasts with his ten claws, dragged her closer to him, and spread her on his bamboo bed.

"True to the words of the diviner, she became pregnant. Her ten years of waiting were over. It was the hottest news in Amawa. Her husband ordered her to do nothing but rest. He told his other wives to take turns serving her food. It was also during her pregnancy that Ezeagwọ died. She was grateful that she'd met him before his death. Life was so sweet for her until I was born.

"The day I was born, according to my mother, when she pushed me out, the midwife screamed her head off. She ran out of the hut leaving my mother naked and bleeding. It was the senior midwife that finished off the delivery process, all the while screaming, 'Arụ eme!' My mother did not ask any questions. She lay there recuperating her strength. When the midwife finished cleaning me and handed me over to my mother, she cried out of our hut. My family members trickled in one by one. They rushed out one by one, reiterating the midwife's cries, 'Abomination!' My mother said she pressed me to her skin. After all, Ezeagwọ drew her ears. If it was just my skin and hair color, which is, by the way, the first of its kind in this village, it would have been better. But I had, still have, both a penis and a vagina.

"The next two days saw her caring for me alone as other women feared me. By the third day, she glued herself to her window, hoping Dibia, the herbalist, would not come. But he came. Accompanying him was a teenage boy, carrying a lidless raffia coffin. Like Dibia, he tied a red lappa across his waist. White chalk drawings decorated his body. Between his lips was ọmụ leaf. He dropped the coffin in front of my mother's hut. Everyone in my family and even beyond gathered around.

"She heard when Dibia said to her husband. 'Go and bring out your wife and that abomination she delivered that we may proceed to cleanse this land.'

"As requested, she tied a white lappa from her chest down to her knees. She shrouded me in a white cloth and pressed me to her breasts, crying. Her husband came into her hut, his face looking as if he wanted to cry, his shoulders slouched. He held her hand and led her outside.

"Dibia pointed at the coffin. 'Put it in the coffin.'

"My mother obeyed. According to her, I wailed, reaching out to her but she was not allowed to touch me again. The coffin carrier raised the coffin with me in it and placed it on my mother's head. She carried it and cried all the way to the stream, accompanied by the silent villagers. She was supposed to drop me there and allow me to float away to the other end: the forest of the dead. But she could not bear doing that to me, not after all she went through to have me. She did not know how she would sleep at night knowing that she left me to cry and starve to death. She knew she would die if she did that. So, in a flash, she decided that fighting for my life was better than living in regret. She sped off with the coffin on her head and ran as fast as her legs could carry her. The coffin carrier ran after her, in close pursuit by the rest of the villagers. My mother ran very fast with no destination in mind. She would have run toward Ezeagwọ's shrine, but he was dead. She kept running until she came across Ekwensu's tree mapped out with ọmụ branches. She ran into that space. Every other person chasing her stopped outside, afraid to take another step. My mother snatched me out of the coffin, knelt before the tree of Ekwensu, and raised me. She said I was surprisingly quiet.

'Ekwensu, the god of terror, I bow down in worship. Here, take this child of mine, as your own, and protect. Do not allow any harm befall your child!'

'No! Kedụ ihe ị na-eme!' her husband screamed.

"But my mother spoke even faster before the arrival of Dibia. Others stood around dumbfounded, their hands on their chest, or mouth, or head.

'Arise, Ekwensu, let all your enemies be scattered.'

"She said some people ran away, tripping over each other, when she said that. She paid no attention to them. She still cried to Ekwensu.

'Strike with leprosy anyone who tries to harm this child. We offer allegiance to you, Ekwensuuuuuu!'

"It was at this point that Dibia arrived. He shrieked and spat in utter disgust. Shaking his head, he looked at her husband and announced. 'Osu ka ọbụzi! Outcast of the worst kind! Avoid them like a bed of scorpions. You heard the mother!'

'Hei!' everyone screamed shaking their heads.

"They walked away one by one after Dibia. But my mother's husband fell on his knees and cried like a child. He could not even touch my mother. The men of his age-grade helped him up, told him not to cry like a woman, and led him away.

"Though still a freeborn, my mother could not return to the village without me. So she came to this land and settled.

This is where she raised me. We plant everything we eat here because nobody will sell to us even from the osu market. We make our clothes here. We are very self-sufficient. She named me Nnemeka which is a combination of 'Nne' a feminine name, and 'Emeka' a masculine name.

"When she died, seven years ago, I buried her over there," Nnemeka said, pointing at a mound of caked sand.

The goats blared and the chickens clucked. The sun shone in full force, yet under the tree, it was cool. Nnemeka grinned. The king scratched his eyebrow. Nwigwe shook the water gourd, squeezed his lips, and gave the gourd to the guard.

The king cleared his throat. "Your mother is a hero."

Nnemeka smiled.

"So, what do you do with your time, apart from planting?"

She smiled again. "I play with nature. I am an intensely creative person. Sometimes, no, most of the time, I go into the forest. I gather leaves, bones, and anything that interests me. Also, I sneak into the village in the very early hours of the morning to collect cow dung."

The king chuckled. If only the villagers knew. "What do you do with the cow dung?"

"Things I like to call 'shit faces.' "

"Shit faces?"

"I could show you."

"Please."

She led him and his son back to her smelly hut. He looked at all the different faces she made on the dried cow dung. One even depicted a face from Ezeagwọ's shrine—the one with the cashew nut eyes and groundnut shell lips. She painted spines, femurs, skulls, gourds, and stones. She made colors from flowers, fruits, leaves, and vegetables such as carrots and beetroot.

Though clueless when it came to paintings, the king could not help but admire Nnemeka's "shit faces."

He dragged in fresh air after coming out of Nnemeka's foul -smelling hut. "Where do you get those human bones?"

"The evil forest or under Ekwensu's tree."

The king could not believe his ears. Who gave her the effrontery to go to Ekwensu's tree and retrieve the bones from a condemned corpse? Was it because she was Ekwensu's slave? He decided against asking her. If she could enter the evil forest and come out, then Ekwensu's tree was child's play.

He pointed to the hut beside hers. "And who has that hut? Your mother's, I suppose?"

"Yes."

"What do you now use it for?"

Nnemeka smiled impishly. "Your Majesty, it is best not to know."

"Well, you have aroused my curiosity. I'd like to see inside."

"It is better if . . ."

"I insist," he ordered. "Please," he added, afraid to offend Ekwensu.

She nodded and led them to the hut. "Because my mother gave me life, I decided that even death was not enough to separate me from her. So, two years ago, I decided to return her life to her. I always eat in this hut and converse with her. Besides, Local Woman needs someone to talk to," she said with a smirk.

The king rolled his eyes. She unlocked the door and let them into her ossuary. The stench he could deal with, but not the full skeleton of Ugomma, daughter of Ozi, wife of Nwogbo-keke, sitting in one corner of the hut. It was painted in bright colors, and covered from its ribs to its femur in a piece of clean, white, cotton fabric. In its hand was a raffia fan. A white fabric went around its skull. Nwigwe made for the door, but the king held him back. When they went back outside, Nwigwe vomited.

Nnemeka stood impassive as if saying, "I warned you, didn't I?"

* * *

Now, five years later, the villagers stand before the king, asking him to banish Nnemeka. He wondered what must have made his good friend scream and run from her hut and into the evil forest. Did Ekwensu possess any of her bizarre shit faces? Or did her mother's skeleton talk? Would she come back from the evil forest this time? Would he get a chance to redeem himself of his cowardice and absorb Nnemeka and *ndị osu* back into the community? But a question kept nagging at him, and this, he asked the villagers, when they stopped making noise.

"Why did Nnemeka run out of her house? Did anybody go to where she lives to find out what chased her away?"

Everyone fell silent.

Virgin Ronke

RONKE SUNK IN the passenger's seat, her mind crumbled like dry bread. Though her eyes were whitish-red as the flesh of ripe sweet *agbalumo*, a fruit not fruit enough for fruit salad, they were dry. Her mother's bangle-laden hand clutched the steering wheel; her veins so visible, so thick, Ronke feared they might crack her mother's skin. Yet, Ronke dared to attempt one more plea.

"Mum, don't do this, please."

Her mother looked at her, scorn darkening her green pupils, the ones Ronke inherited.

"Mum."

Her mother snuffled, her eyes focused on the road. Ronke closed her eyes and sighed.

"You want to disgrace me, Ronke."

"Mum, I am innocent."

"Then let us find out."

Ronke worried deeply about who was doing the finding. She rubbed the diamond ring on her middle finger. Laolu's smiling face flashed before her. Ordinarily, her round lips would have pulled back through the contours of her heart-shaped face, threatening to slide into her hair. But today, she stayed impassive. Her mother parked the car.

She turned off the ignition. "E jeka lo."

Ronke left her butt glued to the seat in defiance of her mother's orders. She stared at the hospital's logo: a cross. It took an unkind tap from her mother before Ronke got out of the car. She carried nothing, no phone, no purse, nothing. She waited for her mother to grab her bag and lead the way. The receptionist grinned on seeing them. Ronke did not smile.

The receptionist curtsied. "Good morning, Mummy."

"My daughter, how are you?"

She curtsied again. "Fine, ma."

"Good morning, Pastor Ronke," the receptionist said.

Ronke bobbed her head.

"I hope Doctor Adeyomi is . . . ah, Laolu!"

Laolu bowed before her, his hands on his knees. "Good morning, Mummy."

She rubbed his back. "Dide, dide, ọmọ mi."

Laolu obeyed and stood erect.

"Is your father around?" she asked.

"Yes, ma."

She walked away. Laolu went to Ronke and put his arm around her. She rested her head on his chest, and he rubbed her bohemian wig.

"Laolu, please, make them stop."

He kissed her hair and led her away from the reception. Her legs felt as if she was wearing stone shoes.

"Laolu . . ."

"Ronke, baby, please. We have discussed this. Let's just get it over with."

Ronke was a hair's breadth closer to breaking the prison wall behind which she had locked her emotions. "Not your father,

Laolu, please, any other doctor, but your father. They will listen to you. Tell them, please."

"I can only trust my father with this, baby." He stopped and ran his forefinger from the root of her nose to its tip. "You look beautiful."

She allowed him to lead her to a chair. He told her he would be right back. Ronke rubbed the diamond ring. She remembered the night she came back home, clutching her Bible, to the angry faces of her parents. Her mother had asked her where she was coming from. She said church. Her mother called her a liar. Ronke knew then that something was about to spoil. Yet, Ronke insisted on her story.

"I went for outreach."

Her mother looked her up and down as though Ronke was disgusting. "You want to disgrace me, Ibironke? Eeh? Have you forgotten who you are?"

"Mum, I went for outreach after church."

"Ah!" Her mother threw her hands on her head. Her green eyes looked drunk in abhorrence. "O ti pa mi o! Ronke, you have killed me!"

"Get lost, Ronke," Ronke's father said in a most disgusted voice.

She went to her room, her heart pounding like heavy rain pelts on a zinc roof. She locked her door behind her with the key and bolt. She took her "vitamins." For six months now, that was the first thing she did whenever she got home. She closed the blinds and turned off the lights before she took off her shapeless skirt. She was not wearing any underwear. The Man Buying Tampons in the mall told her he loved that she wore no undies while they were doing it, standing in the darkest corner of the car park. He asked for her number afterward. She walked away. He shouted after her to at least tell him her name. She did not look back. "Don't you care to know mine?" he said.

He should have been the fourth person that night had the second man not rebuked her in the saving name of Jesus. The first was The Pharmacist Whose Head Was Shaped Like an Avocado. He was alone where she entered to buy nothing. She lied that she wanted to check her BP. He took her to the wooden-boxed-out office and told her to wait. By the time he came back, sat beside her, and told her to roll up her sleeve, she grabbed his hands and pushed them on her breasts, her brown eyes on his. Her nipples were as strong as *iyere* seeds. She stopped looking at him because she did not want to remember his face. When she saw his penis bulge like dough rising in the oven, she raised her shapeless skirt. She could not even remember the name of the pharmacy.

Ronke felt something cold on her hand. She shuddered. But it was just the can of chilled Coca-Cola that Laolu bought for her. He put his arms around her and rubbed her shoulder. She looked at his handsome face, which was repainted with the demeaning color of pity.

"My dad will be with you soon. He is performing surgery."

She nodded and took the drink.

He kissed her hair. "I will be right back."

She nodded. He walked away. His broad shoulders and his legs, as long as a giraffe's neck, reminded her of the first person she voluntarily did it with. She met the man she named Mr. Giraffe at Jabi Lake Park where she had gone to think it through. At first, when she saw Mr. Giraffe's silhouette approaching her, she thought Laolu had found her because she had ignored his calls all evening. She needed to think of her life, her future, her God. She sat on her car hood by the lakefront, in the darkest part of the park, asking God why He had made a caricature of a whole her, a USA Ivy Leaguer, a pastor in the making, the only child of the General Overseers of Return to the Cross

Church. Why did He disgrace her in His house, her hands and legs splashed on the ground like the crucified Apostle Andrew? She remembered being in God's house, alone, preparing her sermon. Suddenly, hands pounced on her, her mouth was gagged, her eyes widened to the sight of five masked men all wearing brown hooded sweaters. One of them pointed a gun at her head and cocked it. They promised to distribute her brain, cube by cube, on the three thousand seats in that giant church should she dare slither again. Her tears burned her cheeks when she knew that they were about to take what she had reserved for Laolu. They plastered her on the altar. Two men held her hands; two men spread her legs. They assigned numbers to themselves. Number one felt like a broomstick inside her. Number two felt like a pestle. She must have passed out. When she opened her eyes, they had evaporated. She was alone, lying on the altar, well-dressed, one would think she'd simply decided to sleep there. She stayed there for a long time, eyes closed. She asked God to take her life now. Now! He did not. She finally peeled herself off the floor and went home. She avoided that altar for two months. Her thoughts were as irritating as a bunch of wet kinky hair stuffed to the brim in a toilet bowl. She vomited day after day until her stomach felt scraped and white. She bore all of this alone, sometimes going off to a silent airy place as if the breeze could sweep away her anger, her disgust for herself. Then she did it with Mr. Giraffe. She hoped it would shield her from the memory of the Hooded Hoodlums. She hoped it would feed her denial of rape. It did not. So she tried again, believing that one consented sex was not enough to mask the rape. She took one nameless man per night and as days added up to months, she was able to take three men per night. She slid deeper and deeper into darkness from where she no longer saw what the Hooded Hoodlums had done to her.

Ronke heard her mother's husky voice. She had not noticed when her mother sat beside her. Her mother looked her up from head to toe and clucked her tongue. Ronke ignored her mother and focused on the sweating can of cola Laolu had given to her. She remembered sweating profusely after doing it with Mr. Giraffe, rushing into her car, driving away. The next day, she bought a blonde wig and brown contact lenses to hide her conspicuous green eyes. It was after six months of plucking men like leaves from a tree, night after night, that her parents noticed that all was not standing well. Ronke decided not to go out the next night after her parents raised suspicious eyes. She read her Bible, showered thrice, watched a movie, but outside kept calling her. It echoed her name like a person shouting in a cave. The sound of her name bounced from one rock to the other and back into her ears. She picked up her car keys. In the car, as usual, she wore her brown sunglasses, brown contact lenses, and blonde hair. She wore her alternate personality. She stopped at the red light. He came to her window.

"Gala, Lacasera! Gala here! Sister, you no go like chop Gala?"

The Yoruba accent was not lost on her. She did not take in his face. But his chest was firm and his thighs looked tight. She tested his knowledge of the Yoruba language.

"Kini oruko ibi bayii no?"

He grinned. "Ah! Sista mi! The name of this place is Ahmadu Bello Way! The express long well well . . ."

She held up her hands before he said more. He went mute. She beckoned him to come closer and bend his head into the car. He did.

She whispered right into his ear, "Ṣe you go like fuck me?"

He shuddered and stepped back. "Blood of Jesus!"

She panicked. The red light still reflected on her glasses. She was afraid that he would raise an alarm. "I'll pay you," she muttered.

She saw the veins on his forehead relax. "I will buy all the gala and lacasera you have."

He looked at the traffic light. She followed his gaze. It was twenty-five seconds left. The Gala and Lacasera Seller called out to The Walnut Seller. Both of them entered her car when the light turned amber. The Walnut Seller asked where they were going.

The Gala and Lacasera Seller said, "Make we carry aunty go somewhere. She go pay us."

Ronke felt a bit afraid. This was strange, even to her. She stayed on the long expressway with dead street lights and parked under a canopy tree by the sidewalk. She stayed in the car while both men got out. The car reeked of sweat.

"Aunty na ten ten thousand you go give us o," said the Gala and Lacasera Seller when they came back.

"No problem."

They did it there, standing by her car, shielded by her car, the tree, the dark. They were fierce. They each had two rounds, yet she wanted more. She lay on the grass, did not mind if a snake was taking a rest, her legs as open as they had been on the altar of God. These two hawkers went the third round each, this time slower than the other rounds. They were breathing fast, but Ronke did not feel as though she had started. They fled. They abandoned their merchandise, forwent their pay, and fled, their heels touching the nape of their necks as they ran. Ronke raked herself up, wiped her tears, dusted her hair and body, flung their goods out of her car, and drove home. She did not have the patience to remove her look when she parked her car at home. She just wanted to get to her room and take a shower and wash their filth away, maybe masturbate to a gazillion orgasms. But her parents were waiting for her in the sitting room. Her mother was sobbing. Her father paced, his hands clasped behind him. On the stool before them was her Ziploc bag filled with empty cards of contraceptive. How did they find her well-hidden "vitamins," she wondered. Her legs stopped functioning. Her father moved his nose up and down repeatedly. Ronke knew she stank of sweat.

She stayed close to the door and curtsied, greeting them. Her father pointed at her and pointed at the floor closest to him. Ronke's feet skated to a few paces from her father.

"Where are you coming from, Ronke?"

"Outreach, Dad."

It was loud, the slap, it came down hard. One of her contact lenses fell from her eye. Her mother gasped and covered her mouth. Ronke bent to pick it up. She felt as though a strand of her hair was pulled. When she raised her head, her father was holding a weak stick, as small as a toothpick and her wig.

"Ah! Ronke! Idi?" her mother cried louder.

"Who have you been sleeping with, Ronke?" her father asked.

Ronke shook her head.

"Tani o je, Ronke? Tani? Who is he?" Her mother wiped snot from her nose.

"Where did we go wrong by you, Ronke? Where? We gave you everything, Ronke. We have been good exemplary parents. Why, Ronke?"

Ronke had never heard her father sound so vulnerable. It did not sound like the voice of the Bishop he was, who at church commanded angels down from heaven. His eyes were dry and as pink as the pink lake of Senegal. His voice sounded fluid. For the first time since the rape, Ronke cried. She hated herself. She had never seen her mother cry before. She hated herself for being responsible for her father's dejected look. She wanted to tell them. She wanted to say the truth, but what justification did she, the future church's General Overseer, have for sleeping with random Abuja men for over six months? How dare she, the fiancée of the most sought-after bachelor in their church, be promiscuous? So she lied.

"Mummy, emi ni virgin." She tipped her forefinger on her tongue and raised it to the heavens.

Her mother vomited a disgusting, provoking, sarcastic laugh. "Yekpa! Virgin Atilantiki ni! Liar!"

"Mummy, I swear I . . ."

"Ronke," said her father's broken voice, "I am an old man. I do not want to put my name in the book of hell by killing my own child. Take your stinking self out of my sight."

Say no more! Ronke took flight, running like the Gala and Lacasera Seller and his friend. She shut herself in her room and cried till the sun started rising. She felt unkind taps on her leg. She jumped up. Her eyes adjusted to her buxom mother.

"Virgin Ronke, e kaaro o. Get ready. We are going to the hospital."

Ronke rubbed her eyes while responding to her mother. "Good morning, Mummy."

"Sebi, you say you are a virgin?" Her mother folded her arms, the grief from last night had been replaced with scoffing. "Get ready. We are going to the hospital to confirm your virginity. And pick Laolu's call."

Ronke sat there for a good thirty seconds after her mother slammed the door behind her. Virginity test? Her life came crumbling down before her like an avalanche. Her phone vibrated. It was Laolu.

"Baby, what is this I am hearing? Your mother called my father yesterday. She says she wants to bring you today for a virginity test. She said she suspects you have been fornicating."

Something exploded in Ronke's head. It certainly was not her brain because she was still thinking. But something shattered in her head like a bomb shattering a glass house.

"Ronke, is it true? I was so embarrassed when my father asked me. I assured him that we are still virgins."

She could not believe that her parents ratted her out so quickly and, of all people, to the family she was set to join next year.

"Baby..."

"Laolu, I am innocent."

She heard his heavy sigh, and she felt his relief.

"I know you are, baby. I trust you."

She felt pity. She knew he wanted to believe her, but she did not know if he actually did.

"I don't want to do this test, Laolu, please."

"But why? What are you afraid of?"

"I am not afraid, Laolu. Please tell them to stop, please."

"But why?"

"I cannot do it in your father's hospital."

She heard a milder sigh. "Your parents were quite insistent. And it is only my father I can trust with this kind of test. Don't worry we will see when you come."

As soon as Ronke rang off, she ran to her parents' room and prostrated before her mother. Her father was nowhere in sight, but she perceived the strong scent of his cologne.

"Mummy, please, I am innocent. Please, Mummy, don't do this to me."

"Fi mi sile ojare! Get out from here and go get dressed! You have thirty minutes."

"Mummy, please! Please! Take me to another hospital, Mummy, please!"

"Ronke! Ronke! Get out of here! Now!"

Ronke gathered herself off the floor and walked away, disheveled. She was finished. She knew. She had been conquered, imprisoned, starved. But what worried her the most: opening her legs for her future father-in-law. How would she look at him ever again knowing that he had seen her sex? Why wasn't anyone else reasoning this?

Talk about the devil. Ronke heard her name in the unmistakable coarse voice of her future-father-in-law. Her can of Coca-Cola almost fell from her hand. He smiled at her. She did not smile. She was overpowered by shame.

"Can't you greet?" her mother said.

She mumbled something even she did not hear. She felt someone rub her hands. She turned. It was Laolu. Her Coca-Cola was still there, every drop accounted for.

"Ronke, shall we?" her father-in-law-to-be said.

Ronke sat there. She could not do it. She could not open her legs for this man. She did not know the other men. She knew none of them: the hooded and the hoodless hoodlums. She did not know their names. They were just figures, sticks, to her. But this man here, this was the violation. She considered confessing, but then was that not why she was here?

"Stand up from there, Ronke!" her mother screamed.

"Ronke, it is all right," Laolu said, "just get it done with, okay? I will be waiting here for you."

He got up and lovingly lifted her and handed her to his father. Ronke's head felt heavy. Her can of cola finally dropped from her grip. She shut down. Like a computer program. Ronke. Shut. Down. The worst was going to happen anyway. She was going to be violated for the first time in her life, and everyone she loved had set her up for it. When she pulled down her trousers and her underwear, in the examination room, she felt nothing.

It was like painting Zuma rock with a bucket of dust. When she lay on the bed and opened her legs, pulled them backward, she felt nothing. When he dragged his stool closer to her and asked her to open her legs further, the shame finally flooded her, but she refused to be carried away by the tide. She squeezed her eyes tightly shut, and she offed herself. She was still like that when he tapped her.

"You have slept already? Dress up."

He was smiling. Ronke got down from the examination table and started dressing. He looked away, writing something while standing, but Ronke did not care if he was looking at her or not.

"When your parents called me, I could not believe it. But I trust you. Your hymen is as tight as a ten-year-old. You are still very much intact. Your parents will be so relieved."

Ronke did not believe her ears. How was that possible? Did it mean that the past six months had been an illusion? Was she nuts or going nuts? But she said nothing. She was drowning in the storm of rage. Her lungs were filled with rage; she could not breathe. She did not want to drown. She needed the light, a new start. He was still saying something when she walked out, leaving the door open. Laolu rushed to her, smiling, speaking English, but everything that came out of his mouth sounded like Swahili, and she did not speak Swahili, neither did she speak Betrayal. She pulled his engagement ring and dropped it on the floor. The thing protested her ill-treatment by jumping up and down, whining down there. She did not answer his many questions. She did not even glance in the direction of her mother. She walked away into the sunlight.

This Man

THE OTHERS AND I gather in the room of This Man. We watch people file in. They weep. They wipe their eyes. They blow their noses. They look into the box and shake their heads. They file out. Four broad-chested men stand like trees, two on each side of the box. They watch everyone who enters the room. Some of us stand in front of these men and make funny faces. We laugh. We name them Osisi.

This Man, who happens to be the great-grandson of a friend who has crossed over to the other side, stands beside me, unable to tear his eyes away from his earthly form: dressed as if he's going for a bank interview, he lies in a lavishly decorated box; his nose and ears are stuffed with cotton wool. This Man is now one of us.

A middle-aged woman with a big stomach, dressed in black like the rest of them, comes in, wailing. Two other women hold her while she counts her steps and drags her feet as if there is a ripe boil between her legs. The baby in her stomach sucks its fingers and swims. We see these things. This Man's heart leaps for joy as he pushes his head into the woman's stomach and tickles the baby. In one quick movement, the woman with child frees herself from her escorts, clings to the box, and raises a leg as if she wants to climb in. We laugh. This Man turns to us, forehead creased, eyes wrinkled, lips turned down. We lower our heads and feign sadness. Then he climbs into the box and lies on his body. Again, we burst into laughter. One of us says to him, "Ofeke, fool. No matter how hungry a man is, he cannot eat his own shit." He sits up on the body, staring at the pregnant woman until she leaves.

This is when the four men we call Osisi proceed to close the box. As they push down the lid, This Man pushes through it and sits on top of the box. Does he not know that no matter how sharp is the cutlass, it cannot sever smoke? That's what we have become: the four elements. The others go to join Osisi in carrying the box, leaving only This Man and me. This Man stands there, his shoulders slouched, his head lowered. I rub his back.

He looks at me. "Why is this happening to me?"

I squeeze his shoulder and nod my head toward the door. If only he knew how lucky he is.

Outside, the box is placed on a bench. Some of us sit on the sand and fold our legs. Some hover on trees. Others sit on people's laps. This Man goes to sit on the box, his eyes on the woman with child. The scent of frying meat and tomato mixes with incense. Mourners flocking here do not care about the dead man but for the food and drinks that will be shared afterward. We know these things. We see them all the time. Hungry people are everywhere squeezing themselves under the shade of the thick cloth that covers the top of four, long, metal poles. Those who see no space there stay under the trees. These humans behave like congealed palm oil. Do they think that they will melt if they stay under the sun?

A man wearing a big cloth—*what a waste of fabric!*—stands behind a table that has two burning candles on it, and he speaks to the people. His big cloth is the color of onions, and he always opens his palms right after he says the word "pray." There is singing, drumming, clapping.

"When a man's coffin is placed before the altar of God," he says, "his head is meant to be facing the crowd such that if he sits up, he's looking at the crowd. But for priests like us, it is the other way round because God is the one to judge priests."

This Man turns and peeps into the box as if to confirm that. The others like me start laughing again. Why are these newcomers always so naïve? Many of us used to be like that. I beckon to him and tap the ground beside me. He shakes his head. So I go and stand beside him.

"How did you die?" he asks me.

I tell him I died during the war. When I died, I sat staring at my body, clueless. Blood flowed from my head, turning the brown earth to dark red. I did not sit forever moping, no. I went to the village to see my family. It was good with them until the day I saw one stupid boy in the bush with my teenage daughter, rubbing her thigh. She did not stop him. I slapped his head, but, alas, I'd become like smoke. Not waiting to see if they will do the thing or not, I rushed back to the bush and attempted to revive my body. I looked at the deep gash on my temple. I figured that since it brought me death, if I fixed it, maybe it would bring me life. But I could not even touch it. I looked at my bound ankles and wrists, swollen from congealed blood and gray from death.

I roamed around and tried to make friends. I met other people, who like me, died in the war. One told me he starved to death. Another told me that she was running from air strikes when she rushed into a palm-frond-bale house. The only other person hiding there did not notice her, and when she tried to touch his stomach, her hand came out through his back. Panic seized her. Still, to be on the safe side, she waited for the shelling to stop before she crawled out of the hideout. She ran around in the streets in utter denial, but she passed through people instead of bumping into them. In a state of disbelief, she retraced her steps to all the places she'd been during the shelling until she found her body, blasted to pieces.

There is this one story that made me thank the gods for how I died. The man, unlike the rest of us, said he was captured by the soldiers, gang-raped every night, and made to clean and cook every day. He died the day the soldiers forced his jaw open and another soldier defecated into his mouth. He choked on the shit and died.

I heard these stories and consoled myself that I would not be here for long. I hoped to repair my body and go back to my family. Each time I looked at my smashed temple, I remembered how the soldier looked into my eyes, as though he were looking at a poisonous reptile. He slammed the butt of his AK-47 into my temple. My head exploded in pain. His ribs were slim and his stomach sagged as if stuffed with a three-legged pot. He raised his hands, thin as stalks, and again pounded the butt of his gun into my temple as if he were pounding palm kernel shells. The last thing I saw before catching death was the red-black-green flag, which had the symbol of a blazing sun sliced in half. The flag that promised us freedom, consolation, hope.

I roamed the streams, forests, and hills. I visited the spirits of infants who live in udala trees. I had a chat with the spirits stationed at every traffic junction. I lingered near my home. I watched my twelve-year-old son go from looking gaunt to his stomach becoming as big as that of the soldier who killed me.

I saw him run after a cockroach, slap it tenderly, squeeze his eyes shut, raise it to his mouth, and eat it; I ran back to my body. There had to be a way to revive it. When I got there I could not recognize what I saw. My eyes cried maggots. Maggots dripped from my nose as mucus. I did not take a second look at my belly. My body had grown too unfit to be willed back to life.

*　*　*

Ala, the goddess of the earth, has had her body opened up, waiting to receive her child back to her belly. I hold the hand of This Man as we escort the box to its new home, beneath the soil, into Ala's belly. I wonder why they waste so much money on a box when a raffia mat will do—whether mat or box, Ala never rejects her children.

This Man holds my hand, gawping at the diggers, and says, "That's the end. I'm gone."

But it is not the end. I do not tell him this because he is among the lucky ones. He is about to die the good death. We wait until the diggers completely cover the box in a mound of sand and then we leave the grave.

His family puts tubers of yam in the back seat of the prayer man's car and a hen in his trunk. He grins and waves goodbye.

This Man's brothers drag a goat to an old man.

"You did not even ask me how I died."

I do not know how to tell This Man that I don't care about how he died. He's dead.

I focus on the old man. This Man keeps talking to me, never mind that I am not listening. Because of This Man's incessant talk, I do not hear the best part of every burial, the only prayer every ghost needs: the prayers over the goat. I see an agile man cut the rope on the goat's neck, severing This Man's ties with the living world. A heavy rush of wind almost throws This Man down. I catch him.

He looks up. "What is happening?"

We see a raging, spinning, upside-down cone of radiant cloud, like a blinding tornado. The more the cloud spins, the windier it becomes. This Man is too busy looking at the blinding cloud, so I do not call his attention to the two men carrying the dead goat and trailing blood from its sliced neck to This Man's grave. As soon as the blood touches his grave, the swirling intensifies in this spinning cone of cloud. The swirling begins to form an oval shape like a hollow giant egg.

He claps excitedly. "Jesus has come for me! I made it!"

He grabs my hand and points toward the light. "I can see my grandmother."

I envy his blessing, but I try to be happy for him. He is not the cause of my misfortune.

"There's my great-great-grandfather. These are my ancestors who died even before I was born." He looks at me. "Why are they here?"

I want to cry. Why can't it ever be me, leaving? I squeeze his palm and say, "They have come to take you home."

"To where? Heaven?"

"It should be. But they are taking you home to the land of the ancestors. The blood has opened a path to eternal life for you."

"Which blood?"

I point to the trail of blood. His eyes brighten. I can tell he's happy. He looks at his forefathers, beckoning him to come. He drags my hand, but I pull back.

"Come with me," he says.

I shake my head. "I hear that a goatskin will be ready for you to sit on when you get there. Go ahead. Don't keep your family waiting."

I walk away. I turn back and see him looking at me and then at the light as if he is confused about whom to follow. I move my palms back and forth signaling him to go. I take care not to repeat my glance. I focus on the men who are squeezing the dead goat into a basin to carry to the house of the oldest man in the family. I am still looking at them when the light disappears and everything becomes tranquil. I go to the others like me, whose shoulders are hunched and heads lowered. I tell them to cheer up. They do not say anything to me. They melt away from the funeral. I see the Ụmụada, the married daughters of the land, dancing and singing songs in honor of This Man. Then I see some men lead a cow out of the compound. I know they are taking the cow to where the goat's body is headed.

As I watch them drag the cow away, I remember when the fattest cow I had ever seen was killed for my uncle, Mazi Awele. His children took the cow to the house of the eldest man in our family. They made a show as they passed through the village so that people could see the honor they were giving to their dead father. People knew that their father would be a big man in the spirit world. When they arrived at the elder's house, they all broke kola nut to give thanks. A cow that has been called the name of a dead man must be killed. Mazi Awele's children couldn't be there when their father was slain, so they left. The butchers blindfolded the cow before killing it so that Mazi Awele would not know who killed him the second time.

Watching This Man's relatives take the cow away from his compound, I know that, like Mazi Awele, This Man is going to be a big man in the land of our ancestors. I, and the others like me, can never be like This Man. We know this. It hurts us.

*   *   *

They took our bodies away from us in the most brutal ways. For some of us, our bodies were poured into shallow graves as if they were planting us, not burying us. For some others, like me, we were left to rot on the soil where we bled to death. Stray dogs fed on our bones. Nobody killed a goat for us so that we could join our ancestors. So we linger, neither dead nor alive. The light eventually came for a few of us. We knew their families had remembered them and done the right thing. Others, like me, have been forgotten, washed away like regrets.

"No victor, no vanquished" their government said. The joke of it! We are the vanquished. They turned our bodies into delicacies for worms and food for Ala. Our bodies made their soil fertile for farming. Yet they say no vanquished?

A child who says his mother will not sleep should be prepared to stay awake. Since they turned us to the sleepless dead by denying us access to the next life where the dead rest in peace, they too should be prepared to stay restless. We do not allow them find the progress they seek: ever. We don't just curse them to fail, we enforce the robust failure that we cause. We empty a drum of sand into any effort they make at progress, shattering it before it even has life. *Onweghi ebe eji azụ eje*, you cannot go anywhere while walking backward.

If one plucks fruits with the intention of filling his sack, he falls to his death under the tree. We drive their leaders to covetousness and watch them kill their country. We prick their leaders' bodies with illness so that they can squander taxpayers' money abroad on treatment.

A man in a cave would learn to make fire from stones. We learned how to influence humans. We follow them when they assemble to pass bills into law. We stand close to them and watch them scratch their hand, beard, or head. We slide into them, through the opening the scratch creates, and confuse their minds. We do not allow them to pass reasonable bills. We are there during the elections. With so many of us in the room, they do not need that air-puffing box that they hang on the wall; everywhere becomes cold. They scratch hairs; we slide in and ensure that the elections are rigged. We will not allow them to elect a person with a genuine commitment to power. We are in their churches, markets, mosques, prisons, courts—everywhere. They walk through us countless times and all they feel is a tiny chill.

There is nothing any of us can do about the past, but we will never rest until we find rest on the other side.

Ọsọ ndụ anaghi agwụ ike.

He who runs for his life never gets tired.

Jee gwa kwa ha!

The Coffee Addict

ACHINA SMELLED OF dust. Her trees, houses, even people's hair and lashes were coated in the dusty film and odor impregnating everything. The white signboard that read NATURAL STREAM, EZEKORO was blanketed in dust. But Ezekoro had no smell. The dry dusty winds that had infiltrated the town felt distant to the windless calm that surrounded the stream. Tall trees towered into the sky, stopping the sun's blaze halfway. Mgbeke had enjoyed Ezekoro's serenity while reading beside the natural pond—that slice of Ezekoro stream assigned to women. The uppermost branches of the dustless bamboo trees stuck together like intertwined fingers, creating a canopy over the calm waters. The sound of water unpacking itself from rock to pond was euphonious. Mgbeke unscrewed the lid of her plastic container of coffee grounds and inhaled its sublime scent; she rarely drank coffee, but found comfort in its aroma. Then she prepared to climb the steps, counting them as always. At one hundred-and-one, she knew there were one-hundred-and-forty-four more sandy steps before making it out of there. She was spent. The books in her bright orange backpack weighed on her spine. Her calves quivered. Her thighs itched as if they fought each other for space. She dug her fingers between them and scratched until her skin stung.

"What is your name?"

"Blood of Jesus!" Mgbeke screamed, the blood in her head dropping into her stomach like a stone into water.

The barefooted woman, who had appeared from nowhere, moved her right palm swiftly as though to catch something. She smiled. Her incisors and canines must have gone hiking. What remained of her teeth was as red as the dust on the untarred Achina roads. Mgbeke's mouth was agape. No sound emerged from her quivering lips. The hair on her skin stood on end, not from the swaying rustling leaves, from fear. She made to run but could not move her legs.

"Blood of Jesus," said the Woman amiably, intertwining her fingers. "It's good to see you."

Mgbeke looked around, wondering if The Woman had flown down from the bamboo trees. The lappa tied across her chest, Mgbeke had no doubt, was white in its former life. She had an M-shaped hairline, and her hairstyle was long curved *isi owu*. It reminded Mgbeke of the crown of hair Chimamanda Ngozi Adichie wore at the 57th BFI London Film Festival. But the similarities ended there. The Woman's skin was dry, cracked, and grayish. Ugly was a merciful way of describing her.

"Sorry, what did you say?" The Woman asked.

Mgbeke turned away when The Woman leaned closer. The miasma of dust hanging around The Woman made Mgbeke sneeze.

"Oh, my bad," The Woman said, and she smiled.

Her smile reminded Mgbeke of the deadly stainless-steel smile of Jaws from the James Bond movies.

The Woman threw something invisible at Mgbeke. "Check if your voice is back now."

"Aaaah!" Mgbeke screamed.

The Woman, at the speed of light, closed her right palm, and with it went Mgbeke's voice.

"I did not warn you before," she said, shaking her closed palm. "If I release this voice and you dare scream or attempt to run, I will pin you to that ground and leave with your voice. Is that clear?"

Mgbeke nodded briskly. The Woman threw her fist, opening her fingers simultaneously, toward Mgbeke's face. Mgbeke tried her legs. They moved. She marched in place to be sure she was free to move. Cautious enough not to shout, Mgbeke squeezed her eyes shut, snapped her fingers, and prayed.

"I bind and cast you in the mighty name of Jesus Christ!"

She opened her eyes. The Woman's eyebrows were slightly raised, her lips pressed together, her forehead creased. Mgbeke knew her prayers were futile.

"Who are you? What do you want from me?"

"Children of nowadays," The Woman said, facepalming and shaking her head. "What do we say to our elders?"

Mgbeke took deep breaths. She felt a compelling, benign aura around The Woman. Looking down, she noticed The Woman's toes were spread out on her feet as though they were avoiding each other. The Woman's big toenails were black. On The Woman's big right toe was a thin pink line of dead flesh that looked as if a tight shoe had suffocated that portion of her foot. Mgbeke's mother, Mgbeke's two siblings, and she had that same birthmark. Mgbeke felt emboldened.

"Not today," Mgbeke replied.

The Woman flashed her incomplete teeth. "Ọkwia? Wait, I'm coming. Let me go and call the god of death so that you will tell them yourself."

Dread blanketed Mgbeke with goosebumps. It's either this strange woman had watched *Game of Thrones* or she would indeed call the god of death. Whatever it was, Mgbeke did not want to find out. "No, no, please!"

The Woman's expression oiled with concern. "You don't want to tell them again?"

Mgbeke curtsied and greeted her like she would greet her mother's people. "Nne, ndenne."

The Woman giggled and clapped. "Ezigbo Nwa. I will have to teach you some manners before you go."

Mgbeke curtsied again, not knowing what else to do.

"Let's go find the answers that brought you here," The Woman said, walking toward the stream.

Mgbeke hesitated. Crickets and birds chirped.

"Blood of Jesus, don't waste my time."

Mgbeke had come for answers indeed. She had not uttered her intentions to anyone. No one even knew where she was. Mgbeke became convinced that The Woman was a ghost, not a mystic with paranormal powers. A cool breeze blew past her. The fear that first struck her was evaporating. She turned and followed The Woman down to the stream. Mgbeke unscrewed the lid of her plastic container of coffee and sniffed.

"Why do you keep doing that?" The Woman asked.

"I'm a coffee addict."

The Woman glanced at her. "A coffee addict or a coffee-scent addict?"

"It's the scent that I like."

The Woman laughed. Her laughter rang out like Mgbeke's mother's. Though Mgbeke felt somewhat safe with The Woman, she approached her next question with caution.

"What is your name?" Mgbeke asked, in her softest voice.

The Woman rolled her eyes. Mgbeke dug her palm into the pocket of her jeans and produced her phone. The rush of light from the screen made her squint. It was past six p.m.

"Set your blue light filter instead of squeezing your eyes like someone looking at the sun. That too much light is not good for your eyes, especially at night."

Mgbeke dragged down the phone's notification panel. She clicked on the blue light filter and her screen turned a sepia tone.

"Thank you," she said, burying her phone back into her pocket. "How come you know a lot about modern things?"

The Woman eyed her. "You plan to enter for Writivism this year?"

The question, the knowing, did not come as a shock to Mgbeke this time. The Woman had twice now reached down into Mgbeke's vault and plucked her unuttered words.

"Why do you ask?"

"Because you sat over there the whole day reading Writivism shortlisted and winning stories."

Mgbeke looked ahead of her. The steps before them appeared endless. She was already tired. Mgbeke unscrewed the lid of her plastic container of coffee and sniffed. She offered the container to The Woman. The Woman waved her hands dismissively. Mgbeke closed her container and returned it to the side pocket of her backpack.

"I don't have a sense of smell."

"What a pity," Mgbebe replied. "But do you have a heartbeat?"

"If I have a heartbeat will I be a ghost?"

Mgbeke felt so small and unintelligent.

"What is your favorite story in Writivism?" The Woman asked.

"Caterer Caterer."

The Woman chuckled. "Pemi Aguda. I like the story too."

Mgbeke stopped herself short of laughing at the way The Woman murdered Pemi's surname. Had she not known better, she would have thought that Pemi was Igbo. "Aguda" came out sounding like Àgụdà, an Igbo word that would literally translate to "let the tiger fall."

"How do you know her?"

The woman raised her brows at Mgbeke. "But Caterer Caterer is not what brought you here."

"True."

Mgbeke jumped over a smashed snake. It must have been trampled upon countless times. She abhorred snakes. She could not even look at a picture of a snake without having nightmares afterward. Once, during a sleepover at a friend's, she dreamt that a cobra bit her. There were five of them in the room. All Mgbeke could remember was the dream. Her friends filled her in on how she jumped up and flew over them. One of the girls ran after her, caught her, and pinned her to the wall, praying aloud in tongues. It was her voice that finally woke up Mgbeke to the scared wide-opened eyes of her friends all staring at her. But she had two strange dotted marks on her wrist: the exact place the snake in the dream bit her.

"Why did you come here, Blood of Jesus?"

The steps were fewer in number now. The end was in sight.

Mgbeke sighed. "The Valley of Memories."

The Woman clasped her hands in utter delight. "Ah! Frances Ogamba, our sister. You know that if you spit from Mbaraorie Achina, it can land in her father's house in Akpo."

"I know."

Death had always scared Mgbeke. Yet, there she was following a dead woman, wondering what her former life was like and how she died.

"Sickle cell anemia finally snatched me away at ninety-nine years." The Woman smiled lopsidedly. "But it found me a ready, fulfilled, happy great-grandmother."

Mgbeke fell in love with this ghost before whom she felt so seen. The Woman held Mgbeke's palm. The Woman's touch was cold. Her grip was firm. It made Mgbeke recall the day her mother gripped her palm and dragged her home for fighting with a boy at school. "You cannot fight at all," her mother scolded when they got home. "How dare you fight a boy? He can kill you. You don't have the same strength as your mates. Your condition limits you!" Mgbeke recalled crying, holding her palms, not sure anymore of what hurt: her hand or her mother's last sentence.

"She means well, your mother, she means well. But your condition does not limit you."

Mgbeke squeezed The Woman's stiff palm and said, "You don't look ninety-nine. When did you die?"

"Sixty years ago."

The Woman looked at her and smiled. Her canines resembled fangs. Mgbeke was no longer sure if they'd been there all along.

"Why did Ogamba's story bring you here?"

"As if you don't already know," Mgbeke said.

"Well, they need to hear it from you."

Mgbeke trembled. Did The Woman mean the Ezekoro deity? Were there other ghosts hovering around? She sucked in air and shrugged. "I came here because I want to know too," she said in a loud voice. "Like Frances Ogamba, I too want to know what my former life was like. How did I die? Was I male or female? I want to know everything."

They had gotten to the pond.

"You might want to urinate now. The next journey is not a small one," The Woman said.

"I don't feel like it."

"Well, go and squat there and urinate," she said, pointing to the side.

Mgbeke looked at the flatland where The Woman pointed. She could not imagine pulling down her jeans while this woman stood there watching.

"Eh, Blood of Jesus, look here."

Mgbeke turned. "Argh! Blood of Jesus!"

Mgbeke covered her eyes with her fingers. The woman had the strangest pubic hair ever. It was in sandy-brown dreadlocks. It was so long it touched her knees.

"Now, go and bend that your yellow yansh and urinate."

Mgbeke obeyed, feeling stripped of her justification to feel shy. When she was done, she washed her hands in the pond and wiped them on her jeans. She stood beside the woman, looking at the water and the silt underneath.

"Now is a good time to bring out that jotter and pen in your bag."

Mgbeke took off her backpack and placed it on her sneakers to keep the wet sand from staining the bag. She retrieved her jotter and pen and put her backpack over her shoulders again. The Woman gently pulled Mgbeke along by the hand. The pond parted when they stepped into it. The fine silt became dry and slanted down as if forming a staircase. Mgbeke did not recall where the pond ended and where the new realm began. A village scene stood before her. It was a sunny day. Women sat on the bare ground. They wrapped a lappa across their chests, and it was draped over their calves. Their wares were arranged on the mats before them. Naked little children littered the marketplace. Almost everybody sold the same things: ugu, ube, oranges, okro, red oil, kola nut, maize, uzuza. Mgbeke started scribbling things down. A young girl, whose chest was unclad like her mates, walked past. She was carrying a bowl of oranges that were as small as her breasts. She piled the oranges beside an old woman whose chest was also unclad. The young girl left carrying oranges.

"Why did she exchange oranges for oranges?" Mgbeke asked.

"Different varieties, different taste."

"And the breasts? What's up?"

The Woman chuckled. "Unmarried girls must leave their breasts bare. Prospective suitors need to see what they are bargaining. But married women must cover their purchased bodies. Old women may or may not cover theirs. But most old widows like to leave their breasts bare."

"And what if you are old as I am and cannot find a husband?"

"Impossible! Girls are married off before their breasts sag. If no young man bargains for your hand in marriage, you'd get married off as a second, third, or fourth wife to an older man."

One buxom woman sat on a stool. Her wrists and ankles were laden with bangles. Her hairstyle was some strange shape pointing heavenward. She seemed to be dishing out orders because she was continuously pointing. Teenage girls, their breasts too perky to flap, ran around following the directions of her finger.

"She is called Omu. She is a queen in her own right, but she is not the king's wife. This market cannot open unless she says so," The Woman said.

Mgbeke wrote that down. They walked past the marketplace to quieter areas. Huts designed in nsibidi lined the streets. Farm animals stayed confined to pens. Branches of palm fronds and yam skins lay spread out before goats and sheep. A woman sat on a mat, surrounded by two bare-chested girls. They were plucking palm nuts from its bunch. A little boy, wearing only a loincloth, joined them. Another woman held the hand of a girl whose breasts were as small as udara seeds. The girl's spare hand was busy shielding her head from the strokes of the stick the woman pelted on her.

Mgbeke pointed at the flogged girl. "The black sheep of the family."

The Woman hissed. "Nonsense! The wool on a sheep cannot become black simply because the sheep behaved badly."

They walked past three young men in loincloths, hoes hanging on their shoulders. They passed a woman applying something from a black gourd-plate on the hair of a sitting woman. Mgbeke went closer. The hair cream was congealed and smelt like palm kernel oil. She caught up with The Woman by a mango tree laden with fresh, big, pinkish-green fruits. A young woman, tying only a small lappa on her waist, folded her arms across her belly. Her hairstyle was bold all-back cornrows. She looked shy. An older woman was crouched down next to her, writing something in the sand. Her long lappa was knotted under her armpit. Her hairstyle resembled The Woman's. Mgbeke went closer to the mango tree. The woman, crouched on the ground, wrote something like this:

"What is she drawing?" Mgbeke asked The Woman, scribbling.

"She is writing. She is telling the girl that she likes her and she wants to marry her. She wants the girl to have babies for her."

"Oh, lesbian couples."

"Listen attentively," said The Woman, stiffly, "a woman can marry a wife in Igboland. This woman might be a rich childless widow or a rich childless divorcee. She will assign male sexual partners to her wife. Her wife would bear children who would answer the name of her woman-husband. In fact, Omu cannot marry a man. She marries women. They are not lesbians."

"But how do you know? Love does not acknowledge biodata. So if two women marry and live together, what else is the definition of homosexuality?"

The Woman stamped her foot. "They. Are. Not. Lesbians."

"But how do you know?" Mgbeke insisted. "How do you know what happens behind their closed doors?"

The Woman shook her head, hissed, and walked away. Mgbeke kept pace with her. They walked past a group of men sitting on a mat. While some hugged their knees, others had their legs straightened out. Gourd cups boiling white froth stood before them. The men laughed and even patted each other's sweaty backs sometimes. Their hairs were hats of afro, and their jaws, bells of beards. Mgbeke and The Woman walked past an elderly man, standing beside a teenage girl, pointing at a vast expanse of land. The Woman told Mgbeke that the man was showing his daughter the land he had bequeathed to her.

"I thought females don't inherit lands in Igboland."

"Blame the white man for that," The Woman said dismissively, angrily even.

Mgbeke scribbled in her jotter. They passed by farmlands, void of people, rich in furrows and plants.

"You sound like a feminist," Mgbeke said.

"All Igbo-born women of my time were feminists. It was your Bible that began to teach them how to be less."

Mgbeke smiled. "I'm a feminist too."

"No, you are not."

"Excuse me?"

The Woman stopped walking and crossed her arms. "How many male authors have you read?"

Mgbeke searched her memory. "Wole Soyinka, Okey Ndibe, Chigozie Obioma, umm . . . emm . . ." She knocked her index finger on her temple.

The Woman smiled. Her available teeth were no longer rusty but yellowish. "I did not ask you to name your friends."

"They are not my friends."

"Of all the hundreds of books you have read, you cannot even mention five male authors. You don't read male authors because you hate men."

"I don't hate men. I just cannot tolerate them and their bloated ego."

"You hate men, Blood of Jesus, tell yourself the truth. You are not a feminist. You are a misandrist."

Mgbeke clenched her teeth. "My name is Mgbeke."

The Woman walked away. Mgbeke unscrewed the lid of her plastic container of coffee and sniffed. Sighing, she followed The Woman. Overgrown grass crowded the pathway, swallowing some of the brown sands of the path. It reminded Mgbeke of guava with pink flesh. A hefty rat scurried on the nearby garden plot. Cocks crowed. Flies buzzed. Goats bleated. Maize stalks rustled. Mgbeke remembered when she lay on a hospital bed three weeks ago. The ward reeked of Izal and Dettol. An IV line was connected to the back of her arm. The IV bag was filled with blood, AA, A+ blood. She gripped her copy of Ayobami Adebayo's *Stay With Me*. Although she saw herself in those pages, she forced herself to keep reading. The death of Sesan resonated with her. Sickle cell crisis was the reason she was always admitted to hospital. Her mother sat beside her bed, saying her rosary. Her ward mate's mother screamed and dashed out. The book dropped from Mgbeke's hand. Her teenage ward mate was in distress. Her chest rose, stayed that way for a few seconds, and then fell. Every time it fell, Mgbeke willed it to rise again. Mgbeke's mother stood in front of Mgbeke, obstructing her view of the dying girl. The girl's mother came back with doctors and nurses. A nurse rolled a blue hospital bed screen and shielded the girl's bed. Mgbeke saw her mother's grip on her rosary tighten. She shut her eyes. Even when the girl's mother's howls rent the air, Mgbeke kept her eyes closed. Grief, regret, and silence are identical, conjoined triplets. Mgbeke uttered no word for the three days she spent there. It could have been her, she thought. She was older, sicker. She was a scared thirty-seven-year-old. She was afraid of getting married and bringing a child into the world who would live their life on the edge every day. She was afraid of real life. Books were safer.

"Here we are, Blood of Jesus."

The Woman's voice and cold hand snatched Mgbeke out of melancholia. They were on a large farm. Women and children sprinkled across the farm combed the soil with their hoes and sliced blades of grass with their cutlass. Sweat cooled the soil. The air smelled like the aftermath of rainfall even though the ground was dry. A woman, probably in her early fifties, dragged sweat with her fingers from one side of her forehead to the other. The sweat drizzled on the ground. She wiped her finger on her lappa and dropped her hoe. She dug her fingers into her cleavage and brought out a wrapped leaf. She unwrapped it. With the back of her thumb, she scooped some brown substance and fed her nostrils. She sniffed in, rubbed her nose, and sneezed. She wrapped up the leaf and returned it to her cleavage. She combed the soil again for a few minutes. Holding her waist, she dragged herself to the nearby Ashoka tree. Her skin was the color of ripe mangoes. She sat under the tree, brought out her wrapped leaf, and sniffed again. Using her index finger to press down one of her nostrils, she blew catarrh out from the second nostril. She rested her head on the tree trunk. Soon her eyes closed.

Mgbeke leaned closer to The Woman. "What is she sniffing?"

"Utaba."

"Hmm. She seems addicted to sniffing snuff."

The Woman scrunched up her face. She looked like someone who was sneering at a stinking person. Mgbeke saw The

Woman's eyes dart to the plastic container of coffee in the side of her backpack and then to her face. The Woman's lips parted into a lopsided smile before she turned her attention to the farmers. Mgbeke stood frozen. She looked at The Woman's head, at that M-shaped hairline. The woman sleeping under the tree had the same hairline. It was the same hairline Mgbeke had. Mgbeke stared in disbelief at the sleeping woman, piecing the puzzle together. They both had celestial noses and that pink line of dead flesh on their big right toes. She felt dizzy. She pressed her feet to the ground and held her head. Mgbeke unscrewed the lid of her plastic container of coffee and sniffed.

A black snake slithered toward the sleeping woman. Mgbeke held her flushed cheek, her eyes wide open. She hugged The Woman, but it felt as though she was hugging cold metal. It seemed the snake wanted to climb the tree but was prevented by the spread-out body of the sleeping woman. It slithered to her back. A scream was what followed. The woman jumped up, wriggling, trying to touch her back. Mgbeke felt a twinge on her back. She jerked, sucking in her stomach, her chest out, her shoulders pulled back. The Woman did not shake. As the snake slithered up the tree for the life of it, a teenager pointed at it and raised an alarm.

"Ọ kwa agwọ o! Ọ kwanu agwọ o!"

Panic erupted. They all rushed to the screaming woman.

"What kind of snake is it?" a woman screamed at the frozen alarmist.

"Echi eteka!"

Echi eteka, tomorrow is too far. Mgbeke had heard that once bitten by Echi Eteka, tomorrow is too far for a change of status from human being to corpse. Three women and three teenage boys carried the snakebite victim. Hoes, cutlasses, blades of grass, heaps of soft fresh soil were all that remained on the farm.

Mgbeke kept looking up the tree to see if the snake would rear its ugly head. Her tongue felt dry. Her back hurt. The sun bit into her skin. Something cold touched her shoulder. She jumped.

"Let's go," The Woman said.

Mgbeke stayed very close to The Woman, scrutinizing every step, wary of green, brown, whatever color of snakes, skinks, lizards, reptiles. The Woman led her to a large sandy compound. There were many huts scattered around all decorated in nsibidi. The woman whose back had entertained a snake lay face down on a bamboo bed in the compound. An elderly man whose hair was as white as the lappa on his waist circled the sick woman. She had been stripped down to her waist, a black stone on her back, a bulb of onion with teeth marks beside her face. Another man sitting on a stool close to the sick woman tried hard to look impassive, but the deep lines on his forehead betrayed him. Three children rolled on the ground, weeping. Among them was a girl, Mgbeke could swear, who resembled The Woman. Other women and children stood around, shaking their heads, dabbing at their eyes. The elderly man shifted the black stone and rubbed something brown that smelled like a mixture of dust and palm oil on the snakebite wound. He sat on the ground, dipped his hand into his goatskin bag, and brought out a dry leaf. He squeezed it and scattered the crumbs on the wound. He was massaging around the affected area when he suddenly stopped, looked at the man sitting on the stool, and shook his head. Cries bellowed.

"Ready to leave?" The Woman asked.

Mgbeke wiped the tears that had gathered in her eyes. Her head throbbed. She felt short of breath. The Woman held her hand and squeezed. Mgbeke found herself back in Ezekoro stream, almost at the top of the steps. The Woman smiled. Her teeth were complete and clean. Her lappa no longer looked like something that was dug out of the earth. It looked clean and white.

The Woman touched Mgbeke's hand. Her eyes glistened with motherly love. "Mgbeke, nwam nwaanyi, always remember that a person who does nothing about their dream is like a person in a coma: both are alive, asleep, and dreaming. Go now. Tell your story."

Mgbeke's eyes misted. The Woman had finally addressed her by her name and even called her "my daughter." She dabbed her eyes with a finger and addressed The Woman by a name she called her grandmother. "Nnemochie, you did not tell me your name. What should I call you?"

She suddenly felt light-headed. The late evening breeze whipped around her and she was ferried into a familiar realm. She saw many faces that looked like hers and heard sounds that flickered like songs. The Woman's name was whispered over the winds. *Mgbokwo*, it said.

When Mgbeke recovered from her trance, a hush, as dark as the evening, had covered the air. The Woman had disappeared. Frogs and crickets filled the night with their sounds. She inched her way up to the road.

Mgbeke unscrewed the lid of her plastic container of coffee and sniffed.

Caked Memories

KANDUDI OPENED HER eyes to a flood of light, a welcomed contrast from her recurring dream of traipsing through the dark woods, tailing the cry of a baby. Her head throbbed. It was worse at her right temple. It sounded like the incessant, rhythmic pummeling of the pestle on an empty mortar. Each sound came three seconds after the former: *kpom*—1, 2, 3—*kpom*—1, 2, 3—*kpom*. Her vision was blurry, as though a thick curtain of cloud stood between her eyes and everything else. She shut her eyes and inhaled. She smelled disinfectant. She heard the sounds of beeping. She rubbed her hands on her thighs. One of her hands felt heavy as though she had elephantiasis. A very thin material covered her skin and she felt the soft surface on which she lay. She opened her eyes again. They rested on a woman's beautiful smile and honey-colored face. Kandudi felt a grip on her arm. She stiffened.

"It's okay, darling," the woman said.

Kandudi's vision became clearer now. She was dressed in a thin hospital gown. An IV was connected to her arm. She was surrounded by machines. The zigzag lines of the heart rate machine and its constant beeping confirmed her location. She did not know why she was there, but she relaxed her arm.

"Welcome back," the woman said. "I'm going to take your vitals."

Kandudi gawped at the lights. It felt good to see such brightness. The door creaked open, ushering in two females wearing blue scrubs. They smiled at her.

"B.P. one-thirty over eighty-four; temperature, thirty-six; pulse rate; eighty-eight," the woman said.

"Get her a glass of water," one of the newcomers said before turning to Kandudi. "My name is Doctor Chioma." She pointed at the second lady in blue. "This is Doctor Tinu. Your friend here is Nurse Ebo."

Doctor Chioma was saying something but Kandudi only heard a deep-pitched, very loud, draggy sound before she slipped back into sleep.

The next day, Doctor Tinu and Doctor Chioma came back after a nurse had cleaned Kandudi's body, checked her vitals, administered drugs, and gotten her a bottle of water. Pleasantries were exchanged.

"It's good to have you back," said Doctor Chioma.

Kandudi raised an eye and furrowed her brows.

"You have been unconscious for eighteen months now. You were involved in an accident."

Kandudi's eyes almost abandoned their sockets.

"It is good to have you back. May I ask you a few questions?"

Kandudi nodded.

"What is your name and age?" Doctor Chioma asked.

"Kandudi. Thirty."

A line etched on Doctor Chioma's forehead. Doctor Tinu was writing.

"Are you married or single?" Doctor Chioma asked.

"Single.

The lines on Doctor Chioma's forehead moved like those on the heart rate monitor.

"Have you any children?"

Kandudi moved her forefinger from left to right two times.

Doctor Chioma dug out her phone and swiped her index finger across the screen. "Where are you from?"

"Achina," Kandudi replied.

Doctor Tinu still scribbled viciously; her eyes thinned and her lips tightened. Doctor Chioma scratched her forehead. The slight wrinkling of her eyes hinted pity to Kandudi.

"What's wrong with me, Doctor?"

Doctor Chioma held Kandudi's swollen palm, the one with the IV. "Well, some of the answers you gave are no longer correct." She snapped her fingers at Doctor Tinu, pointed at the jotter, and opened her hand. Doctor Tinu handed the jotter to Doctor Chioma, and then Doctor Chioma placed the jotter side by side with her phone. "From my years of experience, I can immediately diagnose, with ninety-percent certainty, that you are suffering from what is called focal retrograde amnesia."

Kandudi rolled her eyes.

Doctor Chioma raised a hand. "It is temporary, I assure you. And as far as amnesia goes, this is one of the best."

The doctor smiled. Kandudi did not smile back.

"From our records, you were brought in here by one Chiemela Ezeudo who claims to be your husband. Your file says that you are Kandudi Ezeudo." The doctor looked up from the jotter. "This suggests that you have lost a part of your memory, possibly a few years back. Also..."

Kandudi stopped listening. She could not be married. Did she not know herself? She remembered when she played *kpakpangolo* as a child with her friends, running in a circle, raising dust. Strangers became friends merely by holding the hand of a friend. How she and Onyinye, she remembered the girl's name, danced in the rain and bathed in the sand. The sand, invisible on her skin, glimmered on her black hair. She remembered when her father died. He went to bed one night and was a rock the next morning. She remembered the cotton wool stuffed in his ears and nose. His skin looked dry and gray as if he had been bathed by the harmattan winds. She also remembered the voices of her uncles quarreling over mundane issues during her father's burial, and her wishing she could use her stony father to break their heads. With her mother, she moved into a small shelter made from zinc roofing sheet. It was like living in a boiling pot. Her memories came back to her, not caked and cracked as a clay wall, but hot, soft, and sweet as fresh bread.

* * *

Kandudi opened her eyes to a man sitting on her bed, rubbing the back of her swollen arm. His eyes were deep brown and his skin was the color of unripe plantain chips. His hair was wooly, black, and low-cut. Neat facial hair covered half of his cheeks, his entire jaw, and the top of his lips. He smiled. His left canine was unaccounted for. She was infected by his smile. He smelled like a lathered rose. He was certainly not medical staff or he would've been wearing scrubs like the rest of them. So who was he? She closed her eyes, scuttling through the disorienting sandstorm of her memory. She was an only child. She loathed her uncles: a feeling that was mutual. Her father was dead. So who was this fine man? She felt his soft, pink lips on her forehead, his beard pricking her. She winced.

"I am so happy to have you back, sweetheart."

When you place a plastic bowl upside down on a hard floor and hit the top with your finger, the sound you would hear was exactly his voice. His eyes had begun to look watery. He avoided her gaze and rubbed her arm.

"The doctor told me you lost a part of your memory. That's where you would have found me, your husband."

He looked at her and smiled. He was so fine. His teeth were the same shape and size, except for the missing one, which made him even more handsome. She did not catch the happiness in his voice. It made her remember sepia-toned pictures. He made to touch her, but she moved away from his hand and sat up on her own. She picked up the bottle of water from the table. He got off the bed, dragged a plastic seat closer, and sat.

"I don't know who you are. Stay away from me."

"I am your husband." He struck his chest. "We are married. I…"

"I want my mother. Stay away from me."

"I have proof!" he said, clasping his hands. "Please, I beg you, sweetheart, let me show you the proof, and then I will leave you to rest. I promise."

Before she could object, he grabbed a white, worn-out, polythene bag off the end of the bed and fished out a stack of photographs. One by one, he fed her the pictures. She saw herself looking beautiful in an off-shoulder, white-floral lace dress. Her mother stood to her left, smiling all her teeth to the camera; and he was at her right, looking fine in a black suit. She looked at him. He was the same person in the picture. He showed her gazillions of their wedding pictures, talking and talking: this is my aunt; that is my uncle; this is Uche, you remember? There was a picture of the two of them in front of a black car he said was theirs. There was another one where she was pregnant, smiling and posing in a house with red cushions. She picked out the furniture, he said. Did she remember the furniture, he asked. He was like a cook, sprinkling salt on stale food to make it tasty again. His words meandered like a stream, emptying into her brain and draining out. His desperate effort to fill her memory only exhausted her.

"What is your name?" she asked.

He tried to touch her hair. She dodged.

He touched his eyes with the back of his forefinger. "Chiemela."

She yawned. "Chiemela, I want to sleep."

* * *

Kandudi turned toward the creaking door. Nurse Ebo smiled at her. Kandudi managed a weak smile, sniffed, and turned away. Nurse Ebo sat on her bed.

"Kandi, why are you crying?"

Kandudi shook her head and pressed her eyelids together for a fleeting moment. Tears rolled down her cheeks. Nurse Ebo set about her business of injecting some fluids into the IV bag.

"Do you feel sick?"

Kandudi shook her head. The headache was still there, but it did not make it to her list of problems. When Nurse Ebo was done, she sat beside Kandudi and held her hand.

"Please, tell me, what's wrong?"

"I am afraid. Who am I? Why is this happening to me?"

Nurse Ebo rubbed her arm. "It's okay, Kandi." She looked at her watch. "This is almost midnight. Do you want us to take a stroll?"

Kandudi smiled, holding the nurse's hand tightly as they strolled to the garden, following the half-moon's light splashed in the gloomy blankets of the clouds like a flashlight in a dense forest. Her thin cotton gown swayed in the direction of the wind. Dry leaves squashed underneath her feet as she walked. Nurse Ebo had plastered an injection to the back of Kandudi's arm and had brought along two bottles of soft drinks. They sat on a cement bench in the garden. It felt cold. Nurse Ebo opened one of the drinks and gave it to Kandudi. She took some gulps, closed her eyes, and allowed the sugary liquid to slide through her dry and bitter throat.

"So, tell me, why were you crying?"

Kandudi scratched her eyes. "I don't know him. But he has been too kind to me."

"Who? Your husband?"

Kandudi shrugged. "I'm not sure who he is."

"But we all are. We all know him. Even while you were unconscious, your mother and he always slept in your room in turns. He paid for all your expensive surgeries. Surely he will not spend all that money if he doesn't love you."

Love. That was exactly what she was running away from. She had been thrown off a cliff like an ordinary biscuit wrap into this world where the only person she knew, her mother, was now dead. Kandudi had felt abandoned by life and love after looking at the picture of her mother's corpse that Chiemela gave to her. He said he'd been attending the funeral when he received the call that his wife had emerged from coma. Kandudi remembered feeling dizzy after seeing that picture. And when she woke up yesterday, they told her that she had been unconscious for two days.

"But why are you afraid of him?"

"I am not afraid of him."

She was afraid of what she felt for him. Was it too early to feel? She remembered when she felt his body touch hers. She stiffened and opened her eyes, but he was only lying beside her and cuddling her. She closed her eyes, her heart tolling like a bell, but she felt at peace. She adjusted to make more room for him on the bed. And whenever he wanted to kiss her forehead, he kissed the scar on her right temple, which was not there in any of the pictures.

"He came one afternoon with his laptop and said he wanted to play a movie for me. It was *The Sound of Music*."

"You hate the movie?"

"It is my best movie ever. And just before the part that always makes me cry, he gave me a tissue. He buys me my favorite flavor of ice cream. He knows me too much."

Nurse Ebo pulled her closer. Kandudi rested her head on the nurse's shoulder.

"Kandi, it's been three weeks. Open up. I have no doubt that that man is your husband. Forget the pictures and focus on the sacrifices he's made. Kandi, you are so lucky. You were brought in here unconscious, bleeding through your cracked skull. You had tiny visible strands of wood sticking to your brain, like a broomstick under someone's skin. You pulled through two brain surgeries. This man waited for you to survive. He is still here. See, I look at you and I say 'what a lucky woman' and here you are being afraid."

Kandudi sighed. "It is not that easy."

"You have amnesia. You will only make your head ache the more if you try to remember yesterday. Just flow with the now. Life chose you. Choose life too. Forget the forgotten memories and create new ones."

The wind was peaceful. Bats clicked. Crickets stridulated. Kandudi knew her friend spoke the truth. She imagined angry water pushing through towns, eroding houses, trees, her mother, and her memory. Life had taken enough from her.

Nurse Ebo tapped her gently. "Drink up; it's late."

* * *

Kandudi left the hospital two weeks later with this fine man whose wind of love blew her off the ground.

When she walked into his beautiful big house, which had double gates and a fountain in front of it, she was first struck that the cushions were black, not red like the ones in the pictures. A smiling girl, smelling as if she'd been immersed in a drum of sweat, came and collected Kandudi's bag.

"Welcome, ma," she said, bowing.

Kandudi smiled. She did not know her.

Chiemela asked, "What are you people cooking?"

"Egusi and pounded yam. The soup is ready. The yam is almost boiled."

Kandudi walked around the house looking at the artwork hanging on the wall and the small statues spread out on the TV top. She remembers being philistine. But what did she know? She heard the voices of children. Since seeing the pictures of herself pregnant, she'd been dreaming of meeting her twins. Chiemela had told her that the boy looked more like her than him, but the girl looked nothing like her. She stood by the door and listened.

"Ainde need the biscuit," a baby voice said.

Kandudi wondered what "Ainde" meant. Was it a name? She wished Chiemela had talked less about himself and been more open about talking of their children. She slowly pushed the door open. She sensed that it was a playroom because of its weird paint of pink, yellow, and purple. But she did not recognize the precious two-year-olds looking at her. The girl sat in front of a train track, wearing an engineer's cap; the boy stood by a corner, holding a teddy. Kandudi's heart leaped for joy. She did not know what to say first. Was she to say hello? Hi? I'm your mother? What was she to say? Chiemela put an arm around her. She rested her head on his chest. The children suddenly came back to life, screaming in glee, running to hug their father. He rubbed their heads and laughed. Kandudi found herself smiling. Chiemela held her closer and kissed her hair. Then he pointed at the children, pointed at her, and said, "This is your mummy."

The boy was silent, clutching his penis through his pants, shaking his legs.

The girl said, "No, she's not."

"Yes, she is. Shut up that talking-talking mouth," Chiemela said and led Kandudi away.

Kandudi felt stung. The little girl sounded so sure. They had Chiemela's complexion. And just as she imagined, the boy had her lips. She saw nothing of herself in the girl.

"I'm sorry about that," Chiemela said.

"Oh, it's okay." She waved her hand. "What are their names?"

She felt his hand on her shoulder stiffen.

"Taiwo and Kehinde."

She looked at him. Taiwo and Kehinde? Those weren't Igbo names. She had no Yoruba person in her lineage. Chiemela rubbed her shoulder, raised his phone to his ear, and moved away.

She wandered into a room. There were clothes neatly stacked in the open wardrobe. There was a Bible on the table and an opened notebook and a pen. She heard sounds of high-pitched laughter coming from the other side of the wall. She rubbed her hands on the wall, which felt like sand. She pressed her ear to the wall, but instead of human sounds, she heard *kpom-kpom-kpom*. She pressed her palms to her ears, yet the nightmare sound intensified. A thin cloud covered her eyes as if she was seeing the room through a foggy sky. Her right temple ached. Her feet felt as if they were being lifted from the ground. Blackness.

* * *

Kandudi opened her eyes and looked to her right, where she knew Chiemela would be. He was there all right, but his chair was far away. He smiled closed-lip at her.

"Oh, you're awake, feeling better?"

Chiemela's voice sounded like a doorbell, but his lips did not move. Was she now hearing things? She turned left and saw a very beautiful smiling woman, lips like a hooker's lips plant, eyes and hair as brown as the Sahara. She was dressed in a pair of black shorts and a green top. Her accent made everything she said sound like someone reading off the items on a list and questioning them: rice, beans, oranges, mangoes? There was no break, no breath, just constant commas. Kandudi thought she must be a swimmer for her to be able to hold her breath that long while talking.

"How are you, Kadi D?"

Kandudi wondered if this woman, who was looking at her, was talking to her. Nobody called her Kadi D. Kandudi turned to Chiemela.

He said, "Kandudi, meet Folasade. She is our landlady. Fola, meet Kandudi."

He looked cowed. He was no longer the lively presence she had gotten accustomed to at the hospital. Tired of looking at Chiemela's greasy hair, Kandudi turned her attention to the grinning Folasade. She wondered why he called her Kandudi instead of the "Sweetheart" she had begun to enjoy. The way "Sweetheart" spun from his mouth, his lips looking as if he was pronouncing the letter "O" when he said, "heart," that was how "Fola" rolled out of his mouth. Her own name, Kandudi, now came out stiff.

"Welcome to my home, Kadi D, Thank God you woke up?"

Her home? Kandudi thought.

Folasade was smiling, but Kandudi did not understand why Folasade was here. Kandudi felt intimidated by Folasade's beauty. Her skin, the color of pineapple juice, was flawless; and she was as slim as the letter T. Kandudi realized that she was counting another's coins instead of her notes. Folasade might have the beauty, she thought, but the fine man was hers.

Maybe it was the way she thinned her eyes or the way her forehead creased that made Folasade say, "Let me excuse you two, Emi, see you later?"

Emi? Such fond familiarity! Kandudi watched her walk away. The space between Folasade's thighs looked like a big "n." Once the door was shut, she turned to Chiemela. He rushed to her, knelt beside her bed, and held her hand. She wanted to pull it away but she desperately needed that sense of belonging. She wanted him to choose her. She needed his affection. So she gripped him tighter. He talked slowly, sounding as though he wanted to cry. He said he went bankrupt to keep her in the hospital. He even sold their house and car. Folasade was an old friend who'd agreed to accommodate them.

"She's been very kind to the children," he said. "They even call her mummy."

"Folasade is Yoruba?" she asked.

"Yes."

The names of the children then made sense to her. Folasade had named them. The deceit! She turned her back to him.

"Chiemela, I want to sleep."

* * *

One evening, Kandudi woke up after a fainting spell. Folasade was there, tending to her with a tepid sponge.

"Kadi D, I'm so happy, you're awake, I'm so sorry, about what happened?"

Kandudi smiled. She was tired. Six months ago, Folasade had banned the use of a pestle and mortar in the house after the first time Kandudi fainted, but someone must have forgotten.

"Sit up, take this, it will help, reduce your temperature?" She helped Kandudi up and gave her the medicine. "Just rest, I will have them make you some food, but don't worry, I've flung the damned pestle, and mortar, so that she will not tell me she forgot?"

Kandudi closed her eyes and smiled, loving Folasade. Folasade had become her friend. Folasade was the one who came to her room to spend time with her. Folasade took her everywhere she went, except work. It was Folasade who tried to make her feel at home, not Chiemela. Her children, Taiwo and Kehinde, did not warm up to her. They called her "Aunty" and insisted on calling Folasade "Mummy." She had made peace with that because Folasade was a good mother. Besides, who could blame the children? Her only worry was Chiemela, who no longer talked to her as often. If she sat with them for dinner, he would not say a word, but she would hear his laughter ring out when he was alone with Folasade. So she opted to eat in her room. Life became lonely for Kandudi. She had been thrust into this new world by a man with whom she had fallen in love but who was afraid to love her and children who refused to accept her. She wished, at the very least, that he did not deny her his missing-tooth smile. His smile made her feel safe. Flames of love glistened in her heart and those same flames scalded her. But Folasade was always there, caring, keeping her company.

Folasade was not there when Kandudi opened her eyes again. She must have dozed off. On her bedside table sat an empty blister pack, an empty tumbler, and a near-empty bottle of water.

She finished the water. She felt dizzy and her head throbbed. She found her way to Fola's room, holding her head. Fola was not there. She held the walls and staircase railing until she reached downstairs. Her vision was as shaky as trying to see through a glass of petroleum. She managed to get to the kitchen, but the maids were not there. She decided to ask Chiemela to go and buy her some pain relievers. She got to his door, raised her hand to knock, but stopped.

"Emi, baby, please, let's go back, to the way, things were?"

"I cannot, Fola. My wife is in this house."

Folasade chuckled. "Emi, we used to love each other, I know you still love me, I know you want me, you can have me?"

Kandudi opened the door. First, they froze. Folasade jumped up from Chiemela's body, scratching her head. Chiemela rushed to Kandudi. She took a step back. At least he was fully dressed. But who are these people? Kandudi wondered. She began to feel that Chiemela had shown her doctored photos. A wave of steaming anger rose in her, not for Folasade, but for Chiemela. Why did he bring her here if he did not love her? Chiemela tried to touch her again, but she inched away.

"Kandudi, it's not what you think."

Kandudi slapped his face. She did not know how hard she hit because she was weak, but she did her best to make it hurt. Her head throbbed. *Kpom, kpom, kpom.* Her vision began to cloud. Yet, she stared at this man who had pressed a sweet-smelling rose to her heart but allowed its thorn to slash the same heart in half.

"Kadi D?"

Kandudi gathered all the phlegm in her throat and emptied it on Folasade's face, and then she turned to Chiemela and hissed, "You bastard."

The thick yellow spit made it look like Folasade had been crying sputum.

Folasade wiped her face and said, "You are an ingrate, Kadi D, I want you, out of my house?"

Kandudi was dazed. She looked at Chiemela, but he had returned to his seat, head bent, fingers intertwined. For a second, Kandudi considered begging, but she thought otherwise. She never belonged here anyway. It was about time she moved on. She staggered out of the room and to the children's room. They were asleep. She grabbed their hands and yanked them out of bed. They started screaming. She dragged them. She felt as if the ground was rising to her ankles. Her steps were slow, but she was moving. She felt someone hit her hands and grab the children from her. It was Folasade.

"What the hell, do you think you are doing?"

The children were screaming, crying.

"I am leaving with my children."

"Your children indeed?" Folasade sneered. "Get out of our lives?"

Kandudi waited to gain composure. She felt as though she was going to fall, as if her blood was swimming in her body like a troubled sea. The babies' cries disturbed and destabilized her. She reached out to touch the children but Folasade slapped her hand away. Kandudi finally lost her balance and fell. She kept stretching her hand for her children. Someone held her waist and helped her up. It was Chiemela. She tried to wiggle free but she was too weak. The children cried even louder.

"Fola, please, enough of this."

"Yes, baby, enough of this madness, I should have been your wife?"

"Fola, please, don't. Stop now."

Chiemela's voice was a whisper. Kandudi thought that had he not been right beside her, she would not have heard him, not with the shrieking of the children.

"No, I will not stop, we were an item, Emi, but your mother would not have me, because I am Yoruba, now look at it, you are still with me, you promised me that you would marry her, only to make your mother happy?"

Kandudi's breath quickened as she listened to Fola's breathless list of words. It made her even dizzier.

Chiemela left Kandudi and went to grab Folasade. She wriggled herself free. Chiemela placed his hands on his waist and lowered his head.

"Now, I still have to beg, for your attention, is it a crime, to be in love with you, answer me, Emi?"

Kandudi's headache skyrocketed. The pestle-on-mortar sound exploded. The screaming of the children increased. Flake by flake the cold memories fell on her.

Kandudi enters her house, carrying her shrieking son. She opens her door and sees a woman on top of Chiemela. Folasade smiles at her. Chiemela rushes to her, saying he can explain. The baby is crying. Folasade tells Chiemela to tell Kandudi of the baby girl she just had for him.

Kandudi held her head and screamed at the top of her voice as her caked memories tumbled down lump by lump.

Kandudi looks at Chiemela. Chiemela tells her to ignore Folasade. Baby is crying. Kandudi lays the baby on the red sofa, pushes Chiemela aside, and rushes to Folasade. Chiemela pulls her back. Baby is crying. Kandudi slaps Folasade. Chiemela stands between them. Folasade slaps Kandudi and pushes them and runs toward the kitchen. Kandudi falls. Chiemela falls on top of Kandudi. Baby is shrieking. Kandudi sees Folasade running back, holding a pestle. Kandudi and Chiemela raise their hands to stop her. Baby is shrieking! Folasade lands the pestle

KASIMMA

on Kandudi's head, kpom-kpom-kpom. *Chiemela screams! Baby shrieks! What have you done, Fola! Chiemela is screaming! Baby is shrieking! Baby is shrieking! Blackness.*
Blackness.

* * *

Kandudi woke up. Chiemela was sleeping on the chair beside her bed. She closed her eyes. She did not want him to know she was awake. No matter what the pictures said, Kandudi now understood that she had become the intruder in a family that should be hers. Folasade could have Chiemela. Kandudi did not care. She would leave, at least for now. She did not care to where. But she would start afresh to bake new memories. She resolved to return for her son when she could afford to care for him.

"Sweetheart, you are crying. You are awake?"

She opened her eyes. Chiemela was on his knees beside her. His wet eyes were the color of bubblegum. Dry, white, thin lines shaped like strands of noodle snaked down his eyes to his jaw. He held her hand. She snatched it back.

"Kandudi, please, we can work things out, please."

"Chiemela," she said, turning away, "I want to sleep."

Life Of His Wife

GLANCING AT HIS vibrating phone, he saw the picture of his wife where she wore a yellow *kirikiri star* ankara dress, which was fitted from the breast to the hips and flowed down to the knees. The name "my darling" was boldly written above her picture. He smiled and picked up the phone.

"Hello, honey," she shrieked.

"Yes, babe," he replied.

"Who is your babe?"

"Okay, yes, my dear sister."

"Who is your sister?"

"Which one do you want? I called you babe, you no gree. I called you..."

"Anyone, abeg. That is not why I called you."

He smiled and relaxed in his seat. He knew what was coming.

"Honey, you took money from my bag."

"Is that a question?" he asked.

"I am putting it to you. How many are we that live here?"

"Four."

"See, I am not laughing with you."

He smiled, suppressing a burst of laughter. Even if her voice was sharp, he knew she was not angry. He could tell her angry voice from her pretend-angry-voice.

"Do the children know what money is, talk less of taking it?"

"Much less take it."

"Whatever, Mr. English. Do the children know what money is?"

"You did not ask me if the children took your money. You asked me how many we are in the house and I said four."

"But, honey, why will you steal my money?"

"Ordinary five hundred naira, I won't hear a word."

"Honey, 'ordinary,' abi? 'Ordinary.' It is ordinary, and you stole it!"

"But, babe, I gave you ten thousand naira yesterday."

"Ehen! How much is it now? Besides, five thousand out of that money is not mine. I borrowed it from someone, and I must pay it back. Also, I owe the plumber three thousand. He is coming today to collect it. How much is left for me?"

"Two k."

"And you took five hundred from it."

"Babe, I came back yesterday and handed you ten thousand..."

"Am I using the money for myself?"

"Wait nau, babe... hold on please."

He picked up his second phone and told someone that he was in the office.

"Hello."

"Who was that?" she asked.

"Azubuike. He is coming."

"Biko, I do not want to have issues with you," she said, hissing loudly. "Don't come back without my money. All these monies are not for me sef. I use them to buy things for the house. I do not know why you just cannot release money. You, I will not see. The money you are working for, I will not see. Ahn-ahn!"

He guffawed. The laughter was so contagious, she began laughing too. Since his wife lost her bank job—thanks be to God—she had turned to a professional thief. She was one step away from wearing a hood, surrendering him with a gun—plastic, wooden, metal, whatever—and collecting his money. Anytime he came back with money, he would wake up to find nothing in his wallet, so much so that he'd doubt if he came home with any money. On top of that, she would come the next morning, asking for money. Sometimes, he would go to the filling station, ask to be served, open his wallet to pay, only to realize that his wife cleaned out his wallet. One night, he pretended to be asleep. He saw her tiptoe in like a thief. She searched his wallet and the pockets of his pants and suit hanging in the wardrobe. After that night, he began sleeping with his wallet under his pillow.

He laughed harder. "Thief. You are angry that you got beaten in your own game."

"Got beaten how?"

"Did you not still steal from my wallet even after I gave you the ten thousand?"

"Steal what?"

"I had about three thousand naira left in my wallet. You see you? I came home with thirteen thousand. I gave you ten and kept three. Yet, you came and stole the three. Now, I have taken only five hundred naira back, let there be peace, and you are there calling me to bring it. Ngwa, give me back my three thousand, and I will return the five hundred."

"I did not go to your wallet."

"Swear."

"The Bible says we should not swear."

They laughed again.

"Abeg, go your way. Thank you for calling," he said.

"Honey, please bring my five hundred naira when coming back, abeg, unless you want to keep vigil this night."

"Okay, bye."

"Wait, why are you chasing me away? Is there a woman there?" He laughed.

"This woman, allow me to work nau."

"Waiti! Please send me back the airtime I used in calling you now, please. They just warned me that my airtime will soon be exhausted."

He exhaled. "Don't you have thousands of naira there?"

"So, you mean you cannot buy me common recharge card?"

"I can. But you have money with you. Go and buy."

"The money is for other things. I will have none left by the time I am done from the market."

He knew, as well as she did, that she was not going to any market, was not owing anybody any damn five freaking thousand, did not call any blessed plumber to fix anywhat. Yet, he humoured her.

"Okay, I will use the five hundred naira to buy the recharge card."

"No o, buy me the recharge card and still bring back my five hundred naira."

They laughed.

"Honey, I am not joking with you," she said.

"Ngwa, save your remaining airtime."

"No."

"Ọginị?"

"Say that you will buy me the recharge card, and you will bring my money back."

"Okay. Agreed."

"Okay?"

"Okay."

"It is a lie. That 'okay' came too easy."

They laughed again. This time, he was tearing up.

"I will do as you have said. You own me, don't you?"

"Do not forget that."

"I will not."

"Ehen, bye-bye."

She rang off. Five minutes later, she called again. He declined the call and called her back.

"Why did you cut my call?"

"What did I use in cutting your call? A royal sword? I declined your call. I did not cut it."

She hissed. "Why..."

"I don't want to buy one thousand naira airtime for you. That's why."

"Wisdom is profitable," he said as they both laughed. "Why did you call?"

"Just to say hello."

He smiled. His heart was warmed.

Worthless Strength

ADAMMA DIED ON a very hot day. The sun was out blazing. The trees stood like corpses in the still air, the leaves on their branches were in a vegetative state. Ikeemewuike, thirteen or fifteen years old, hopped on the scorching sand, on his way to Adamma's family. Gossip is best delivered hot, he thought. He tripped on the furrows left behind by the erosion at Ukpakamanje. He landed on the hot sand and jumped up again. He did not bother dusting off his sandy skin. It was best Adamma's people saw it. That way they would know he was not joking. Ebele village was far, but not today. He made the journey even shorter by rehearsing the name of the village as he was taught by his late mother: A-bay-lay. He was thrilled. Ikeemewuihe, the useless stranger, would be the one to tell the Ezeanwụnas that their daughter was dead. He could not wait to see them fling themselves to the floor and strike their bodies, crying. Bliss! Perhaps they would even really hurt themselves (*please God*). He laughed as he remembered when they laughed at his mother and called her a whore. "You this loose woman with your awusa son, how dare you make noise in this market?" they would say when she fought for the undelivered goods that she'd paid for. Imagine his surprise when he learned that the word was "Hausa," not "Awusa." He laughed. Illiterates! He was still laughing when he heard someone hailing him.

"Ikeemewuihe nwa awusa! Kedụ?"

Ikeemewuihe smiled. His mother was from Ụmụeleke, Achina. His father, he never knew. So he's from Ụmụeleke, Achina. Whatever others thought was their opinion, not his reality. He remembered the day he stopped giving a damn. The day he cried to his mother, begging her to tell him about his father so that people would stop calling him a bastard. She shuddered, her breathing increased, her fingers started trembling. She tightened her legs and pressed her palm to her mouth. Sweat from nowhere drenched her. She pulled herself to their bamboo bed and lay down. He rushed out to the backyard, retrieved a bucket of water and a towel, and ran back inside. He wiped her sweat with the cool water and sang her favorite song: *Oke nke ume nke m nwere, chim adịghị ehi ụra*. And for the first time in his life, the song made sense to him, and it became his favorite song too: *As long as I breathe, my guardian spirit does not sleep*.

"Nwa awusa, is it not you that I am talking to? I said kedụ? How are you?"

He grinned and waved. "Akwaanebereego! Ị ka na-ebe?"

Akwaanebereego clenched his fist and squeezed his lips. Today was Ikeemewuihe's day of laughter, his day of revenge. How great is our God!

"Akwaanebereego, your name follows you. You keep crying for money. That is why you are still poor."

"M wude gị, ị hụ a ihe."

Imagine Akwaanebereego with his knocked knees threatening to catch him and teach him a lesson. Ikeemewuihe laughed harder. He wondered if Akwaanebereego was the name his parents gave to him or was it a nickname? It must be a nickname.

Maybe he acquired it because he always refused to sell his dehydrated agidi and thin pepper soup, made from anorexic cows, on credit. And he was known as the only trader in Achina who had never said, "Keep the change." He must collect his money to the last kobo. Yet, upon, *akwa ọ na-ebere ego*, all his cries for money, he was still poor.

Ikeemewuihe had gotten to Ezeanwụna's compound. Life was normal there. Adamma's mother sat out front, picking ọha leaves. Adamma's brother, Ebuka, patched the tyre of his motorcycle with eba. Uncles, aunties, cousins were littered everywhere, walking up and down, carrying water on their heads, holding brooms, sitting, laughing. He heard her father's husky radio doing what it knew how to do best: disturb the peace.

"Ndi be Ezeanwụna, ekene m unu!"

They looked at him and went about their businesses. Some even hissed. Nobody responded to his greeting. He laughed. What first came to mind was to pick up the stone by his foot and throw it on the grave of their most respected father, Ọchụdo. That would annoy the hell out of them and they would pay attention. But he remembered his mother. He remembered the night he lay on their bamboo bed, sick from the cane and fist thrashing he'd received for pickpocketing. Had it not been for his mother, they would have killed him. But his mother came from nowhere, pushed her way into the crowd, and embraced her son. The villagers stopped the flogging because they did not want to kill an innocent person. But what their hands did not do, their lips did. The villagers called them names. They told her to return her bastard Hausa son to where she got him. Why did she return after she was captured by the Nigerian soldiers and whisked away to Hausaland during the war? Why did she not stay there with her bastard who was as weak and as damned as they? But she said nothing. She held her son tight until they got tired of insulting her and left. She scooped him from the ground, laid him in her wheelbarrow, and pushed him home. One would think that her skin-and-bones body, thin as Akwaanebereego's cows, could boast of no strength. But those who saw her realized that her will, her strength, was fattened. She took her son home, put him to bed, and nursed him back to health: alone. The chemists would not even sell painkillers to her. God would be mad at him for saving a thief, the chemist said. Ikeemewuihe responded to her herbs and soon was able to talk. The first words he said were apologies.

"I'm sorry, Mama."

She smiled. Her voice was as soft as a rose petal. "You have always said you hate your name, haven't you?"

He nodded.

"Why do you think I named you Ikeemewuihe?"

He shrugged and winced from the pain that shot through him. He thought of the day he asked his mother why she had given him such a cursed name, but she acted as though he was not talking to her. He remembered destroying her raffia palm kitchen walls in a state of raving rage. By the time he sneaked in that evening, she had built half of it back. The next day, he finished up the work. Nothing was said about his rash behavior. But he started calling himself Ike, which meant strength, the opposite of his full name. So when anybody called him Ikeemewuihe, he would beat the hell out of the person to demonstrate his strength. It worked. The village children stopped trying him.

His mother smiled. "Ikeemewuihe might mean, when you translate it as a layman, 'the worthless strength, the strength that can achieve nothing' but when you think of it with the brain of an elder, you understand that it means 'strength is not the answer.' So, what then is the answer, my son?"

He wagged his index finger left and right. He was still in too much pain to do anything more.

"Wisdom is the answer. Wisdom opens so many doors that strength cannot open. Had Ojukwu and Gowon been wise, Biafran war would not have happened. My family would not have died. I would not have been stolen away to the North. I could have been a headmistress by now."

He managed a weak smile.

"So do not be ashamed of your name. Wear it with pride. Choose wisdom over strength, and, one day, you will become the president of Nigeria."

He chuckled and winced again. She laughed.

"I'm a thief," he said.

"So are those in office, my son."

He giggled, not minding the pain.

"I know nothing about one plus one."

"The same is true of those in office, my son. If they did, they will not be miscalculating funds. You are a perfect candidate for president."

Ikeemewuihe tightened his hands around his ribs and laughed until he cried happy tears, which his mother lovingly wiped away.

"I stole the money for Ude. He would not be allowed to write the exam if he did not pay. He is the only person who still talks to me in this village. And he is intelligent, unlike me."

His mother smiled. "Hush, my son. Don't explain yourself to me. Don't explain yourself to anybody. Those who love do not need the explanation. Those who don't love you would not understand."

Those words would make sense to him years later when he was in office. But that night, in that stuffy poverty-stricken room, with one window, and dank air, he cried.

"You should stop stealing, you know. They could have killed you."

"I cannot. I am a thief."

"That is what they say, my son. Someone's opinion is just what it is: an opinion. It is not your reality. You tell yourself who you are and the universe will make it possible."

He nodded.

"So who are you?"

"Ikeemewuihe Ezeude, your son."

"Yes, you are my son, my beloved son. But you are Ikeemewuihe Ezeude, the president of the Federal Republic of Nigeria."

He laughed again, breathing hard from the pain. "A useless, uneducated, poor boy in a thick village. How will I become president?"

"See it for yourself, my son. Keep your eyes on the light, on the prize. And always remember the magic words."

"Yes, I can."

"That's my son," she said, and rubbed his head.

He smiled. He did not tell her that he used the magic words when he went to steal, yet, he got caught. He did not tell her that he used the magic words when he tried to climb the mango tree, yet he couldn't. He did not tell her that the magic words never worked. He did not want to offend her. She took some beating for him. He ought to be grateful. If she believed "Yes, I can" was magic, saying it wouldn't hurt. But what hurt was watching her hold her waist and limp out of the room, no thanks to the pelting she received while trying to save him. He clenched his fist and promised himself to make them pay, but his name rang in his ears like udu drum: ike-eme-wu-ihe. That was the day he reverted his name from Ike to Ikeemewuihe.

"Ikeemewuihe, is it not you I have been calling since?" Someone screamed at him, snapping him from his nostalgia.

It was Mama Adamma. Her face was squeezed like a flattened bottle cap. He smiled. His time had come.

"Shị nkene pụọ nweị ma amawa gị anya! Get out of this compound before I slap you! You are surveying this place now looking for what to steal!"

He looked to his right. There was a big stone beside the upturned sand. He wondered whether the stone was at the dead man's head or his feet. The houses in the compound stood sprinkled before him, apart from the one before which Adamma's mother sat, which was to his left. He instantly knew that the stone was at the dead man's feet. It's tradition to bury a person in such a way that if they sat up in their grave, they would be facing their compound. Ikeemewuihe sat on the stone.

"Nwa gị nwaanyị anwụgo."

Mama Adamma became as still as the weather. Ikeemewuihe ticked that box. Ebuka, who was feeding his tire eba, froze. Their eyes locked. They could have as well been Adamma's dead eyes.

"What did you just say?" Ebuka asked.

Ikeemewuihe was looking at Ebuka's bald head when he responded. "I said your sister is dead. Adamma died a few minutes ago."

Ọha leaves went flying in the air. Mama Adamma jumped up, spread her hands like Jesus on the cross, screaming. Ikeemewuihe sat on the stone and watched. This was why he ran all the way here. He wished more people, from Achina precisely, would die so that he could break the news to them and watch them grieve. His mother had been buried like a dog. There was no funeral. Three hours after her death, some men came to their compound and started digging a grave. One hour later, his mother was transported from the hospital to the grave. There was no coffin. No tears. No siren. Even the IV in her hand went down into the grave with her. They covered the grave and left. He wept after they left, spent days and nights by her grave weeping. Nobody checked on him. Ude would have but he had gone off to the city as an apprentice, because the university path closed to him, no thanks to Ikeemewuihe's inability to steal his exam fee successfully. From time to time, hunger swept Ikeemewuihe away to the farms where he stole food. That had been his occupation. Seemed the magic words now worked.

So seeing Adamma's family in turmoil, those running out to ask Mama Adamma what was going on, those asking him to speak, made him very happy.

"Speak before I knock off your teeth. What happened to her?" one hefty man commanded.

"Oh," Ikeemewuihe said, casually, "her husband beat her to death this morning."

Mama Adamma's body dropped to the ground. Another ocean of confusion swarmed into the place. Ikeemewuihe knew he would not need food that night. This was filling. He wished he hadn't been so flippant delivering the news. It was no mere beating. Adamma endured a banquet of fists. She gave up her body when she could take no more. He wondered if he should at least tell them the best part of it, that her husband's people went about their normal business as he knocked the life out of this woman. It was only when she stopped crying and her useless husband knelt beside her, shaking her, that his family members showed concern. But he suspected that Adamma's family would be aware of the abuse she endured from that prick she married: the prick who did not know that *ikeemewuihe*—strength was worthless; wisdom, profitable.

As if someone read his thoughts, a lady cried out, "And she has been complaining of the beating o! We should have asked her to come back! Oh, Adamma! Adamma!"

Ikeemewuihe wanted to bottle the frothing saliva of the convulsing compound and drink it down like a victor's Champagne.

One of the compound doors flung open, so forcefully that the frail wood unhinged. Ifeanyi came out holding a cutlass. He swiped the thing on the ground twice. Ikeemewuihe smiled. He admired Ifeanyi. His thick torso and bearded pimpled face, Ikeemewuihe loved. Someone grabbed Ifeanyi by the waist while another person grabbed the hand that held the cutlass.

"Ifeanyi, odogwu, mba. No. It's not like this."

"That ewu! That goat! That bastard! He killed my sister!"

Ikeemewuihe sat there mentally correcting Ifeanyi that Adamma was his cousin, not his sister. But he was pleasantly surprised. He did not know that Adamma's prick of a husband was a bastard too. Amazing!

"They will come first to inform us. That is our tradition. Drop the weapon for now please."

"Tradition! Tradition be damned! Tradition kept my sister there! Tradition killed my sister!"

She is your cousin for goodness sake, Ikeemewuihe thought. More men held Ifeanyi until they prized the cutlass from him. Yet, they still held him tight. Ifeanyi's chest marched to the rhythm of his heartbeat. Nobody seemed to notice Ikeemewuihe and he liked that. He had stayed in Achina long enough to know her tradition. He had heard and learned so many things while hiding in trees. He was on top of the tree when Amaka's younger brothers welcomed their in-laws to their compound two weeks after she died at age eighty-six. Two of the in-laws came. One stood some meters away from Amaka's father's compound, a keg of palm wine and a carton of beer beside him. The other entered the compound carrying a keg of palm wine. Amaka's brothers and the elders in her family sat outside, facing the entrance of their compound, watching their in-law struggle with the keg he carried, but no one stood to help him. After the ritual of the breaking of the kola nut, the keg carrier said,

"When we married Amaka, it is not the woman that we married, but her ability to procreate. Ọ bụ omenaala. It is our tradition."

His in-laws nodded, chewing their kola nut. The keg of palm wine lay there untouched. Ikeemewuihe was just learning of this tradition.

"So we have come to inform you that your daughter, Amaka, is very sick, and, perhaps, dying."

Ikeemewuihe picked his nose. Were they talking of Amaka who died two weeks ago? Didn't this keg carrier and his one-eyed in-law exchange condolences in the market the other day over Amaka's death? Ikeemewuihe did not understand.

"You have done well, our in-law. You people have been good to our daughter. So we have no doubt that she is in good hands. Go and continue to take care of her. We only ask that you keep us posted," the one-eyed man said.

"Thank you, my in-laws."

Keg Carrier left. He went to the road and met his brother who was still standing there like a tree. Keg Carrier carried the second keg of palm wine while his brother carried the carton of beer. They returned to the elders who had not moved their buttocks. Their story this time was, "On my way home, my brother here informed me that Amaka has died. So we came to inform you."

Amaka's brothers screamed and snapped their fingers and ate their teeth as though they were just learning of her demise for the first time.

"We have brought this wine to beg for your permission to bury her in our compound."

"Our in-laws," one-eyed man said, "we have heard you. Our family and yours have been living in peace as one big family. You have our permission to bury our sister, Amaka, in your compound. Please keep us posted on the funeral arrangements."

Ikeemewuihe had seen that drama play out so many times that he imagined how it would be when Adamma's prick came. Ikeemewuihe spotted the perfect tree from where he would enjoy the show. He imagined their visit. One stops by the road while the prick (*please God*) and whoever else carries the keg of palm wine to Adamma's father's compound.

"Our in-laws, we have come to inform you that your daughter, Adamma, is very sick, and, perhaps, dying."

Then Adamma's family will say, "Hurry and go and bring her here so that we can take care of her. We gave you a living being, don't bring us a corpse. So hurry please."

Then Adamma's prick and in-law will stand there, stammering. Ifeanyi will then fling the door open. This time, the door will give way and fall. The loud sound of the bang startles Adamma's prick and in-law and, in fact, saves their lives. They see Ifeanyi running toward them, bearing the cutlass. They take off, running like student-athletes on the track. The nonentity on the road sees his brothers running toward him and he flees without even knowing why. Ikeemewuihe will then come down from the tree and grab the keg of palm wine by the road.

Mama Adamma's body still lay there, people ran up and down, sprinkling water, fanning her, holding Ifeanyi, sitting on the ground, crying.

Ikeemewuihe laughed, pocketed his hands, and bounced away, telling himself, "Yes, I can."

Ọgbanje

AFTER YOU BURIED your third child, your father, fed up with the deaths, summoned you. You were not surprised, no. You had expected his summons earlier, especially because the deaths of your first two children were exactly the same. Nine days after her birth, your first child went to bed healthy. The following morning, she was as stiff as the frozen chicken you buy from Mama Chigozie's shop. A year later, you welcomed a baby boy, who, on his tenth day, never woke up.

Arriving at your parents' house at dawn, you found them seated on white plastic chairs, arms folded over their chests, lips turned downward, eyes staring at nothing. On the ground beside your father's outstretched legs was a gourd of palm wine, its mouth stuffed with ọmụ nkwu leaves. Your father's walking stick was between his legs. His raffia hand fan sat on his lap. Three tumblers and a thick, green, glass plate with two kola nuts on it were on the stool before your mother.

"Ahn-ahn, why are your faces like rain-battered shit. Ọgịnị?"

"Sit down, my son," your father said.

You dusted the spare chair and sat. "You two look moody."

Your father proceeded with the kola nut ritual. He was in no hurry to thank his gods and ancestors for a new day and for everything else. You kept stealing glances at your wristwatch. When he offered you a lobe of the split kola nut, you declined.

"Agụnna, kedụ?" your father asked.

"I am fine, Nnam," you responded.

"You will have to stop looking at that clock of yours. A man whose house is on fire does not pursue rats."

You rubbed your beardless jaw. "Nnam, you know that I am the only doctor in the hospital. I have to be there on time."

Your father took a bite from his kola nut. "I have called you this morning for two reasons. First," he said, raising his forefinger, "you must get interested in this family's arọbịnagụ and learn the yearly ritual in its honor. I am an old man with limited time in this space. Our arọbịnagụ have faithfully provided us with riches from which you have benefited. Do not let the spirits scrape your mouth on the ground before you start sacrificing to them."

"Nnam, at the risk of repeating myself, I am an assistant pastor and cannot participate in such fetish practices."

Your father looked at your mother.

"It is our tradition," she said. "What is fetish about offering the oracle a white fowl and three kola nuts yearly? It does not stop you from going to church."

You shook your head and looked at your watch. You'd had this argument several times and could spare no patience for it that morning. The loud sound of your father's gulps pulled your eyes away from your wrist. Tiny froths of palm wine seeped from the tumbler. For a brief moment, you felt pity. Your father used to be huge and agile. Now he was all wrinkles and bones. Your mother, once a feared teacher, also had not been spared from the aging process.

"Secondly, Agụ," your father said, now with two raised fingers, "it is about your childlessness. This issue chases sleep away from my eyes. How can I join my ancestors knowing that my only child is childless? Agụ, agwọ nọ n'akịrịka."

"There is no snake anywhere, Nnam. We have had all these discussions before. My wife and I are just going through..."

"Through what?" Your mother snapped. "We have had this discussion before." She mimicked you. "Can you not see that whatever is eating your children is above Western medicine?"

You sighed. Some distance away a cock crowed and the sun rose at a snail's pace. You glanced at your father's feet. His toenails were black, thick and curled down.

"It is not above Western medicine, Nnem. My first son died of pneumonia. My first daughter died of diarrhea. My second daughter..."

"Died of gonorrhea, or is it syphilis?"

"Nnem, my children did not die of gonorrhea."

"I guess it was simple chance that their gonorrhea and syphilis took each of them on their ninth nights on earth."

You snorted in disgust, falling back on your seat and breathing heavily. Your mother clucked her tongue to deride you. You ignored her. It had become bright. The bleating of hungry goats and sheep and sounds of sweeping replaced the howling of dogs. The sounds of praying, singing, and quarreling rose above the rest. You heard a woman scream at a child to get ready for school. You looked at your watch and gasped.

"Nnam..."

"I have told you to stop looking at that clock."

You sighed in resignation. "Nnam, don't worry. I will have a child. My wife will give birth to the one that will stay. We are taking adequate medical precautions now."

Your father smiled lopsidedly. Old age did not hide his dimples. "It is beyond the white man medicine, nwam. A person pressed with watery feces does not walk. I have taken the pains to go and consult a diviner. He confirmed my fears." He cleared his throat and spat out the thick, yellow phlegm. "Agụ, you are having ọgbanje children."

You jumped up. "Dear Jesus! God forbid!"

You circled your hand around your head and snapped your fingers. Your mother shifted her legs as if to dodge the ill you pushed away.

You sat again. "Nnam, please, I am a Christian. I do not believe in all these things. What business have I got with ọgbanje children, for goodness sake?"

"Those wicked and mysterious spirits choose whomever they want."

"But I have had a boy and two girls."

"Who all died the same way, and, I am certain, at the same hour," your father said. "You do not even need a diviner to tell you that you are dealing with ọgbanje spirits here."

Your mother hissed. "We warned you not to marry that thing that you got from God-knows-where. It must have come from her."

Two deep lines appeared on her forehead. But you were not prepared to go down that road with her. No, no, not today!

"My son, a man who removes a woman's clothes does not just stand and stare," your father said. "You must join me to go see Abiankata. He can put an end to this."

"Me?" You struck your chest. "In a shrine? Are you joking? Is this no longer 1994? Or have we gone back to 1915?"

Your mother pulled her ear. "Use your tongue to count your teeth, gị bụ nwa!"

"Nnam, please I have to go. Thank you for your concern, but I cannot do as you have asked. I am an England-trained medical doctor, and I am telling you that my children's problems are purely medical. Our next child will stay. Watch and see."

* * *

You knew everybody in the village watched and listened as soon as your wife's fourth pregnancy became news. You made sure that your wife took every medical precaution. Amalachi did not miss a day of her routine pregnancy drugs. She ate fruits and fed well. You insisted on that. Even your pastor did not bat an eye when you told him you were going to his rival church to seek a miracle. This pastor prayed over a white handkerchief and gave it to you. His instructions were clear. At midnight, spread the handkerchief on Amalachi's stomach and read Psalms 91 and 23. The handkerchief would become a spiritual ultrasound machine, he said. Place your lips very close to Amalachi's belly and speak life to the child. After this, drop the handkerchief in a white basin—he emphasized the white color—and pour hot water on it. Then hold hands with your wife and pray until the water is warm enough to drink. Both of you should drink it. Do this every day until the baby is born.

You also visited a Catholic priest who gave you a rosary after making the sign of the cross above it. He asked you to recite the Chaplet of the Divine Mercy every day. You had to buy books about Catholicism to learn how to say these prayers. You even went the extra mile of placing the rosary on Amalachi's stomach while she slept.

You were always falling asleep in the office. Your body went from chubby to gaunt. Though your wife gained weight, the strain was not lost in her eyes.

The baby arrived. She was so fat that she tore Amalachi's vagina to make more room for herself to pass. Her skin was as smooth as cream. Her eyes were the brightest brown eyes you'd ever seen. She had your full nose and heart-shaped lips. She looked nothing like your wife.

You were certain that this child would stay. She sucked breasts more than her siblings. She smiled often, gave no troubles, and grew fatter each day. These were good signs but you did not let your guard down. You prayed and recited your rosary every morning and night.

While Amalachi slept on the ninth night of the baby's birth, you kept watch. You had to eat kola nut, something you find very bitter, to stay awake. A part of you was afraid that your father was right. The other part of you continued to wallow in denial. You never took your eyes off that baby, not for one second. You said the Divine Mercy Chaplet with your eyes on her. Your ears were attentive to her soft snores. Not too long after that prayer, an eddy of cold air crept through the windows, swirled the curtains. The air whooshed by and you felt slightly scared when a chill on your skin made all your body hair stand on end.

The truth is, there was a presence in that room. The spirit stood close to you, looking at you as if trying to divert your attention from the baby. It had a neck as long as a giraffe. Its body, covered with white hair, was as muscular as a chimpanzee. Its legs were as pink and as soft as a tongue, and its fingers nested together like a sleeping bat's wings. Then, it started shrinking, turning to a human form. Its spider-face turned to that of a very handsome person with bright red eyes and black pupils. Its hair looked like long strands of algae. It had a muscular torso but no sex between its legs. It walked away from you and stood close to the bed. It lifted your daughter's spirit and rocked it tenderly. Then it jumped out of the window with your baby's spirit and turned into a bat.

When you no longer heard your baby's soft snores, you placed your index finger under her nose: no breath. You raised her hand, and it surrendered to the force of gravity. You turned on your flashlight, pulled down her lower eyelid. Her fixated brown pupils stared right back. You stumbled back to your chair. Your head spun like a sewing machine's wheel. When you got a hold of yourself, you looked at the time, 4:00 a.m., about the time your other babies died. Everywhere became still. The curtains stopped waving, the wind stopped howling, and the chill vanished. You stared at the lifeless body of your baby, squeezing the handle of the chair as if to crush it. Taking it in your stride, one deep breath at a time, you returned to your room. You lay on your bed and put a pillow on your head but sleep did not save you. Even when your wife started screaming at dawn, you stayed the same.

* * *

Five months later, you came back from work one night to find your wife crying in the sitting room. You went to the kitchen to look for food but were only met by pots so sparkling, they almost blinded you. You settled for bread and roasted groundnuts.

"Nonye, what is it?" you asked your wife when you went and sat across from her with your dinner.

You were the only one who did not call her by her nickname, Amalachi, a name she got because she loved to eat amala.

"Your mother came here today."

You sighed, knowing what was next.

"It was worse than her former visits. She called me Mamiwater. She said I came to use you to produce children for my spirit husband. She cursed me. She said I will die during my next childbirth."

"What!" You accidentally knocked down the plate of ground-nuts, scattering them across the floor. "My mother said that to you?"

Amalachi blew her nose. "Nobody sells to me in the market. Nobody speaks to me. They squeeze their faces and hide their children's faces when I pass by. They call me names, spit on me, call me ugly."

You went to her and hugged her. She buried her face in your chest and bawled. Tears dropped from your eyes.

"You are not ugly. Don't mind them."

But you were lying. She's ugly. Let's not go into her orange complexion. Not chocolate, not fair, not bleached, orange! She was the only orange person in the entire village. Her ugliness was as acrid as a mixture of chloroquine and bitter leaf juice. Imagine someone drinking this. What would the person do to their face? Squeeze the hell out of it, is that not so? And even spit? Good.

"I cannot continue like this, Agụ."

"Don't worry. The next baby will stay."

She raised her head from your chest, shaking her head. "Go and see Abiankata."

"What!" You pushed her away. "Have you joined them? Have you forgotten that I am an assistant pastor?"

"There are many ways of serving God." She cleaned her face with the flat of her hands. "Christianity is not the only religion. Look at me." She jumped up. "I am a skeleton. Look at my breasts." She raised her shirt and drooped her chest to your face. Each breast was as thin as half a slice of bread and dangled like feather earrings. "They are flat but no child to show for it. I almost died during the last labor. You know how much blood I lost."

"Don't be melodramatic. I will never turn my back on God," you said, dismissing her with the wave of a hand.

Deep lines appeared on her forehead. Her orangeness shone. "Melodrama, is it? Melo . . . Fine. If you will not consult Abiankata, you either take me back to my parents or I will kill myself." She stormed out.

You took it as a flippant statement. But, two weeks later, when a sachet of rat poison surfaced in your rat-free house, you agreed to consult Abiankata.

The next day, before dawn, you went to see your father and narrated your ordeal.

Your father smiled. "You are ready to be my son. I have been trying to tell you this long ago, Agụ. A child dances to the sweet melody of Surugede without knowing that Surugede is the dance of the spirits."

That same morning, you and your father strolled to the house of Dikeọgụ, the abiankata. His sandy compound was decorated with marks from a traditional broom. A teenage girl carrying a pail of water on her head curtsied as she greeted the two of you.

"Thank you, my daughter," your father responded, smiling from molar to molar. "Nwa a ga-alụ alụ! Please tell your father that I am here with my son."

You felt embarrassed for the little girl when your father called her "marriageable."

Your father pulled you closer. "That is the girl you will take for a second wife if this option does not work."

"God forbid, Nnam," you whispered back. "I am not a pedophile."

Your father scrunched up his face and hissed.

"Nweze!" a very deep voice rang out from inside the house. "Welcome. The door is open."

Your father raised his raffia hand fan. "Dikeọgụ! Ekene m gị."

You gave your father a hand as he climbed the steep steps. You parted the worn-out curtain for him and waited for him to enter first.

The deep voice rang again. "Welcome. There is seat o!"

You looked around you. There was a wooden altar lighted by a tiny bulb. It shocked and relaxed you to see the crucifix between the portraits of Jesus and Mary. A huge rosary hung on a nail to the left of the altar.

You nudged your father, your mouth almost entering his ears. "Had you told me that this man is a prophet, I should have come with you long ago."

Your father chuckled and whispered, "He is both a Christian and a native diviner."

You did not believe him. You looked at the brown sofas and wooden table. The floor was covered in a sparkling blue carpet. Nothing suggested that this man was a local diviner. Three curtains at different parts of the house suggested that there were three rooms. Along came a woman with a big stomach, whom you assumed was his wife, carrying a tray. She was all smiles as she asked after your mother and your wife. She dropped her tray bearing a saucer of garden eggs, ose ọji, and two cans of soft drinks. A tall man, who could not be more than forty-four, dressed in a neat police uniform emerged from one of the curtains. He wore eyeglasses and a neat moustache. Even when you heard his deep voice, you still did not believe that he was Dikeọgụ. He shook your hand firmly as your father introduced you to each other.

"You have not touched your kola?" Dikeọgụ said.

"Kola is in the hand of the king," your father said.

Dikeọgụ laughed. "Go ahead. It belongs to you."

You were still quiet. Both of them spoke as though you were absent. You heard him tell your father that he had eaten kola already. You stopped listening. You did not understand what was happening. How did this young man end up as a diviner? You heard them laughing about something you must have missed.

"Why is your daughter at home?"

"That one," Dikeọgụ said, waving his hand. "She got suspended for fighting in school."

"Ewoo."

"And let me warn you, my daughter will go to the university and become a doctor like your son. She is not to get married yet."

Goosebumps ran down your arm. You were very certain that this was what your father whispered to you when you were outside. How then did this man repeat what you two discussed?

Your father laughed. "Of what use is a woman if not marriage?"

"Anyway," he said, hitting the back of his palms on his lap, "my own daughter will be the best woman she can be. When she is educated and successful, you will see how men will fall over each other for a chance to bear the honorable title of 'her husband'."

Your head nodded on its own.

"So let us get into what brought you people here. I am about to go to work."

"Work?" you blurted out.

He laughed, pointing at himself. "Can you not see that I am a police officer?"

You could no longer hold back your questions. "You are not the dibia, are you?"

He shook his head. "I am not the dibia."

You held your chest and sighed in relief. A dog barked some distance away.

"I am Abiankata," he said.

"Are they not the same thing?"

Dikeọgụ laughed. "They are not the same thing. Agwudibia is a native physician. I am a diviner. So if you are sick, this is not the best place to be. Go to Okafor's house."

You pointed at the altar. "You are a Christian, are you not?"

He shrugged. "I cannot boldly go by that title, but my wife and children are Christians. It is the same God but different methods of worship. I go to church occasionally though."

As if he could still read the confused look on your face, he added, "Stop by another day and I shall clear all your doubts. For now," he glanced at his watch, "let us get to business. I am running late."

You rubbed your jaw and nodded. Your father relaxed on the sofa, shaking his legs and chewing his teeth.

Dikeọgụ drew closer to the edge of his chair. "Agụ, I have consulted Nneagwu, the goddess, on your behalf. She told me that you are having ọgbanje children."

You shuddered. You looked at your father who tilted his head slightly as if to say he told you so. You began to think that you were watching a drama unfold. Had your father secretly convinced this educated man to pretend to be a diviner and convince you of the ọgbanje thing?

"Your wife is pregnant, is she not?"

Your stomach turned. You only found out yesterday after you tested her urine yourself. No one except the two of you knew. How then did this man know?

"She will give birth to that baby, a girl. However, I'm afraid she will die like the rest of your children."

Dikeọgụ looked at his watch again. Your father lowered his head and rubbed his forehead. You clutched your stomach, feeling as if you might vomit.

"It is too late to save this one. We will use her to set an example. After her death, I will give you a charm to bury by your house and give your wife a concoction to drink. But, and listen very carefully, when the baby dies, neither you nor your wife should touch the corpse until I come."

You could no longer hold back. You rushed outside.

* * *

Amalachi tried to keep watch with you this time, but she dozed off on the chair beside you. When you confirmed your fifth baby dead, you staggered back to your chair, shaking. You waited until you gained composure before you tapped her softly.

"She's dead. Don't shout and don't touch her."

She still tried to shout but you covered her mouth and clenched your fist. "I said don't shout. Do you want more trouble?"

Her tears ran over your hand. Your wife cried until a few minutes later when Dikeọgụ's voice and bell-staff tolled in your compound. You unlocked the door and went outside. It was no longer the educated policeman that approached your house. The voice, however, was unmistakably Dikeọgụ's. His gait was a tiger's. He was barefooted. His anklets were made of bold white beads. He wore an ankle-length, white, cotton skirt and a white, sleeveless, baggy shirt. He had a big goat-skin bag slung over his shoulder and he did not wear eyeglasses. A living turtle was fastened to his neck by a black rope. He neither greeted you nor responded to your greeting. He entered the house walking backward and straight to the room where the baby lay as if he had been there before. Still reciting his incantations, he scooped up the corpse and walked outside. You held your sobbing wife as both of you followed him. The eerie howling of the harmattan wind threatened to push down the trees and cover everything. Amalachi hugged herself.

Dikeọgụ dropped the corpse on the sand and sat about ten feet away. "Undress her."

You left Amalachi standing alone and carried out Dikeọgụ's order even though you felt as though you were exposing your dead baby to the cold. Her body was still as soft as cotton.

Dikeọgụ brought out a dagger from his bag and pointed it at you. "Lacerate her."

Your legs felt stiff and heavy. You wondered how you could stab your dead baby. Your wife clutched your feet, pleading with you to allow the child to die well at least. You shook your legs free, mistakenly kicking her in the jaw, and took the dagger from Dikeọgụ. Consumed in the helpless rage from watching your children die, you dug the knife into her chest. Blood sputtered out, splashing on your wife and you. You stabbed all parts of the baby's body except her face. You could not bear touching her cute face. Her organs were visible. Tears streamed down your eyes. You could not even bear looking at your wife who kneeled beside your baby, wailing.

"It can hear. Speak," said Dikeọgụ.

You looked around as if trying to figure out where the malign spirit stood. "You evil spirit, you better not come back here! When you go back, tell them that I, Agụ, the tiger, said that if I catch you here again, I will rip you piece by piece. I will gouge out your eyes and chew them raw. I will use your brains for ngwọ-ngwọ."

Dikeọgụ laughed. He produced three bundled ọmụ leaves from his bag, which he gave to you. "Cover her."

You spread the leaves all over the bloodied corpse.

"Set her on fire."

You dashed inside, got a box of matches and a cup of kerosene. As you doused her with the kerosene, you saw Amalachi holding her chest as though she was preventing it from falling apart. You flung the cup, struck a match, and threw it on the corpse. The smell of burnt flesh filled the air. You hugged the wailing Amalachi. Suddenly, you heard Dikeọgụ laughing, his oily face made visible by the fire, and pointing at nothing you could see.

"See them running away. Can you not see them over there?"

* * *

One year later, after obediently adhering to Dikeọgụ's instructions, Amalachi gave birth to a son. You peeped through the window, observing the procedure. It irked you that as soon as Amalachi pushed out your baby, the nurse screamed and fell off her stool. The terror on her face was mixed with utter disgust as if she was staring at a plate crawling with maggots. She rushed to the sink and scrubbed her hands.

You rushed in and looked closely at your crying baby, who was still attached to his mother through the umbilical cord. You recognized the long scars all over the baby's body and even on his scrotum. The longest and deepest scar ran from his chest to his stomach. He had pink patches all over, like someone with vitiligo. You did not understand any of it. He wailed, kicking his legs, reaching out to you.

You clamped the umbilical cord, cut it, and carried your son.

Where One Falls Is Where Their God
Pushed Them Down

THEY SAY, "WHERE one falls is where their god pushed them down." Well, I fell in the church, right at the altar of God. I know I shouldn't have, but then, I'm only human, and my *chi*, my beloved guardian deity, pushed me down.

My chi pushed me down the tunnel of temptation the first day I led the Praise and Worship session in church.

Pastor Dorcas was right there in front of me, eyes closed, hands up, voice raised in worship to God. Maybe it was the way she shook her head. Or the way her black mascara streamed down her ivory face when she cried. The fishing-line-weave choker looked beautiful on her neck, but its beauty could not compare to the splendor of her wrinkled skin and flabby stomach. My eyes darted to her curvy hips. I wanted to run my fingers from her neck to her breasts and then further down. Seeing her up-close for the first time sent erotic chills swimming from my head to between my legs. But I raised my voice higher in worship to God Almighty and enjoined the church to do same. When I eventually stopped singing, the church praying in tongues, she opened her eyes and our eyes met. My heart skipped a beat when she smiled at me. I did not smile back, could not, not with the entire congregation looking at me.

After the service, I stayed glued to my seat. I knelt on the purple carpet, clasped my hands, squeezed my eyes shut, and said the Lord's Prayer. "Lead me not into temptation, dear Lord," I reiterated, "but deliver me from all evil. Should I fall, however, sweet heart of Jesus, please love me still."

Someone tapped my shoulder. I raised my head.

"Sorry to disturb you, Ọkụchi, but Pastor Dorcas would like to speak with you."

I froze. I saw the messenger's pink cheeks and yellow teeth, her red lips moving, but I heard nothing. How could it be that my chi was setting me up like this? I looked left to where I knew Pastor Dorcas sat. She was there, smiling at me. I thought of how I'd walk past all the church members who were sprinkled around the hall, discussing and laughing. A woman with folded arms stood in front of a man in an oversized suit whose hands moved with wild gesticulations. I saw our drummer teaching another member of our choir how to dance *Etighi*. The church was near-empty, but there were people everywhere, hobnobbing. I sighed and grabbed my purse and Bible.

I fell on my knees before Pastor Dorcas. She rubbed my back and asked me to stand. She tapped the seat beside her. I sat. She smiled at me. We eyeballed one another. *The devil is a liar.* I lowered my head.

She held my hand. "Your voice is as beautiful and as graceful as you are."

"Thank you, ma."

I noticed a brown triangular stain on my black, suede, platform shoes.

Pastor Dorcas placed her palm on my lap. "Would you have time to stop by my office tomorrow?"

I stiffened. *Nope, can't do. I will never ever forever come to your office.* "No problem, ma. Say three p.m.?"

"Three is perfect, my daughter."

* * *

At home, the table was set for lunch. I sat in my spot, removed my shoes, and waited. On the Lazy Susan were three big, white, covered ceramic bowls and four metallic, serving spoons. Fried plantains filled another flat ceramic plate. Soon, I heard my parents' voices as they descended the stairs, my mother's deep-pitched laughter, and my father's deeper-pitched laughter. A strong hand squeezed my left shoulder. I turned and smiled at my father.

He sat to my right, his spot. "Ọkụm, you should consider recording a song, you know."

"Thanks, Dad, I . . ."

"May we say the grace," my mother said, her palms opened.

My father and I exchanged glances. The three of us held hands and bowed our heads. My mother always led in the grace before meals.

"Kind God, we thank you for this meal that we are about to receive. We pray you to provide for those who cannot eat. Especially, dear God, Mr. Adekunle, who has not regained his appetite. Thank you for healing him so far, Lord. Merciful God, please take away the life of Mrs. Haruna. It's painful to see her suffer, knowing we can't cure her again. My guess is that you will not heal her either. So why not just put her out of her pains and take her life? And God, for Mr. Onoja, I thank you for his speedy recovery from surgery. At this time, Lord . . ."

"Ahem!"

The sound came from my right. I did not dare open my eyes. I heard a rasping breath from my left.

"Please, God, forgive my husband who is so in a hurry to eat he cannot pray for the afflicted. And may this food nourish our bodies and keep us away from the hospitals. Amen."

"Amen," my father and I repeated.

I ate quietly thinking about the next day's meeting with Pastor Dorcas. Would we be alone? What could we possibly talk about? How would I survive in a room alone with her? I heard my mother call out to our houseboy to get her a bottle of wine. I watched him set the bottle down on our table. I focused on my plate. My mother grabbed the bottle. I heard the soft glugs of the wine into her glass before the bottle touched down on the table again.

"Okuchukwu," she said.

That was what she called me when she had something serious to say. She used to call me Okum. My father has since taken over calling me Okum.

"I saw you talking to Pastor Dorcas after service."

I tightened my grip on the fork in my hand. My armpit suddenly felt moist. I looked at the AC, hanging on the wall behind my mother. The green numerals shone: 16°C.

My father's eyes lit up. "Oh, you met with Pastor Dorcas?"

"Yes," I mumbled, looking at my food.

My mother sipped her wine. "What do you want with her?"

I looked at my mother. Her piercing eyes probed me from over her glasses. I distracted myself with her hair, a mixture of black and gray that touched her shoulders. She caressed the horn-shaped pendant hanging from her neck. Were it not for that pendant, one would not notice the tiny silver chain that blended with her skin, the color of peeled Irish potato. She adjusted her flower-patterned buba gown, using her forefinger and her thumb.

"Okuchukwu, what do you want to do with Pastor Dorcas?"

Her question got me even more troubled. *What do I want to do with Pastor Dorcas? Really!* I lowered my head and stared at the half-eaten rice and plantain on my plate. I heard the frog-in-the-throat sound as my father gulped his water. Then he set down his empty glass on the table.

"Honey, what manner of question is that?" my father asked.

"Did I ask you?"

I looked at my father. He too had gray hairs, but not as plentiful as my mother's. His shoulders were broad and still firm for a man his age. He was sixty-seven, the same as my mother. The clinking sounds of pots came from the kitchen.

"Ọkụchukwu . . ."

"Mum, Pastor Dorcas asked me to see her on Monday."

"Who asked to see who?"

"Oh, Ọkụm, that's great!"

"Thank you, Dad."

"I am sure she wants you to sing at her upcoming birthday party," my father said.

I shrugged.

"Ọkụchukwu, how many of you did she invite to her office?"

I stabbed the plantain on my plate. "Mum, I don't know, please."

The calm way with which she peered at me from over her eyeglasses rankled. It pressed my alert button. It made me imagine that she was in my body, tearing my heart apart, sniffing my brain as if it's a steaming pot of soup, searching for what-I-don't-know.

My father tore a piece of meat from his chicken thigh. "I'm sure it has to do with her seventieth birthday party."

My mother pointed at me. "Ọkụchukwu, go and get yourself a man."

My father chuckled. "Honey, be nice to the girl. She will get married when she finds Mister Right."

My mother tapped the table. "She's not even searching."

I sighed, wiped my mouth, and dropped the napkin. "Thank you, Jesus, thank you, Dad, thank you, Mum." I pushed my chair, carried my shoes, and walked away.

I heard my dad whisper, "You should be patient with this girl." My mother did not whisper her retort. "She should leave women alone and go and get married. Her mates are all married."

I made for my room. As soon as the door was securely locked behind me, I yanked my clothes off my body and dropped on my bed. I spread my legs open like daisies and masturbated. I felt relief and guilt. I began to cry. My mother used to love me. She used to tell me that I was the light of her life.

* * *

The last time things stood well between my mother and me was when I was in Senior Secondary school 2. My parents came on my school's visiting day. My mother pinched my cornrows. She worried that they were too tight. My father told her to let me be. When we finished eating, she asked to see my books and my test scripts. I ran off to my classroom. Students and parents were sprinkled everywhere. I saw a junior girl hugging her mother. Her mother dabbed at her eyes as if she was afraid of letting her tears drop. I smiled. Sometimes I wondered if my mother's tear glands functioned. When her mother died of cancer—after three days of loud, continuous, agonizing, groans—I wept. My mother merely said, "Your tears won't bring her back. Don't cry too long." Even during the burial, I saw Dad struggle in vain to blink off tears. My mother stood there, stone-faced, beside Dad, watching her mother's white coffin lowered into the ground.

On my way out of the classroom, I saw Uchenna. My eyes fell to her breasts, but I quickly looked away.

"Ọkụchi, I've been looking for you. Thank God!"

She held her chest and placed a hand on my shoulder, panting. I only hoped that she did not feel the blood rushing down my head when her hand touched me.

"Where are you going?" she asked.

"My parents are still around."

"Oh, that's great. May I say hello to them?"

"Sure."

I held my books tight. I did not want to yield to the temptation of touching her. Thoughts of last night filled my mind. Uchenna and I had finished studying on my bed. She yawned, rubbed her eyes, lay down, and dozed off. I thought about going to her bed. But I did not want to go down to that hall alone that night, not with the eerie stories of Madam Koi-Koi and Bushbaby that were all the school was talking about. So I lay on my back, beside Uchenna. I crossed my fingers on my stomach, my eyes stuck to my bunkmate's black mackintosh and her Pokémon bedsheet sticking out. I recalled when Senior Olaide touched my breasts last year: the only person to ever do that. She'd invited me to sleep on her bed. In the middle of the night, I felt her hand ticking my nipple left to right like a pendulum bulb. Olaide was our labor prefect. She was feared. So having her touch my breasts, I did not know what to do. I did not know if I should be angry, grateful, afraid, I did not know. I lay there, shut my eyes, and allowed her to fondle my breasts from underneath the blankets. At some point, I began to enjoy it. But I tightened my thighs when her fingers slid down between my legs. She withdrew and turned her back to me. After that night, she still smiled at me, still called me "My Girl," still placed her arm over my shoulders when we strolled. She still gave my class the easiest labor. She still remained my choko, my special friend. But she never invited me to her room again, and we never talked about it. Several times, I built up the courage to tell her that I wanted her to touch me again, but several times, my courage failed me. Olaide graduated.

So having Uchenna lie beside me, I started to shake inwardly. My underwear felt wet. I looked at Uchenna. Her silky nightgown had slipped down her right breast, exposing her pink nipple. In an attempt to cover her, my fingers brushed her nipple. I quickly withdrew my fingers. She let slip an odorless fart, sounding like a boiling kettle. She continued to snore softly. I wanted nothing more than to touch her nipple again. So I turned to my side and fondled her nipple with my index and middle fingers. She stopped snoring. I expected her to hit my hand away, but she turned to me, eyes closed as if she was just turning in bed. Her breasts slipped out of her nightgown. I grabbed them.

Uchenna left my bed at the toll of the rising bell, and now I was introducing her to my parents. My mother smiled at her and focused on my notebooks. My father engaged her in a discussion about schoolwork. When my parents were set to leave, Uchenna joined me in seeing them off to the car. I walked between my parents while she walked beside my mother, her hands buried in her pockets. The pressure from her hands in her pockets flattened her gown against her body so much that I thought the fabric would snap. When my parents drove away, we walked back to the dormitories, silent. Then she held my hand suddenly. We were shielded by an empty classroom. Her eyes were tearful. They looked contrite.

"I'm sorry, Ọkụchi."

I waited to hear more. She stammered a little, then shook her head, and ran off.

I went home during the holiday to find that our house girl had been replaced with a boy, Chidi. I was surprised to see this agile boy, about my age, wearing an apron, and coming to collect my bags from me. I turned to my mother.

"Mum, what of Chinazo?"

"We had to let her go. Inside with you."

I saw my father squeeze my mother's palm. I rushed to the sitting room, stood behind the window blinds, and eavesdropped.

"I am not comfortable with leaving this girl with this boy in this house. It is not safe." He was almost stammering.

My mother was not even sounding breathy when she said, "Just like it was not safe leaving all the house girls with you."

"This is not about me."

"Of course, my decision this time to switch the house help from a female to a male has absolutely nothing to do with you, rest assured of that. But what about your complaints? Are they for yourself or your daughter?"

My father sighed loudly. "Don't put our only child at risk because I made a mistake."

"Mistakes, you mean? Ọkụchi can take care of herself."

I heard the *koi-koi* from her heels, and I ran upstairs. It now made sense to me why she changed house girls as if she were changing TV channels. That was also when she stopped calling me Ọkụm. That was when she started looking at me from over her eyeglasses. That was when I concluded that things were not standing well.

When I graduated from secondary school, I remember telling my parents of my intention to become a reverend sister.

My father grinned. "I can see those Sisters in charge of your school have spat in your mouth, eeh?"

"Why?" my mother asked, calmly.

I had only one reason: the convent flowed with females.

"I like their lifestyle," I said.

My father clasped his hands. "Oh, that's so sweet. Of course, you can join them, if you want."

"She cannot."

"Honey, can she at least try?"

"She cannot. We are not Catholics. She cannot."

Truth, they say, is the salt of a story. I should have told my parents the truth about my sexual orientation that day. But adding ube to vegetable salad simply because ube is a vegetable is sheer foolishness. So I crawled back into my shell.

When I was at university, I tried out a relationship with a boy. When we had sex, I felt as if I had opened my legs like a toilet for him to piss inside me. I pushed him away. It was the first and last time.

I threw my feelings into a bottomless pit and buried myself in the things of God. I joined the choir and got busy with the demanding church activities. Since we are what we think, I thought of myself as someone else, a heterosexual Christian. Until my chi pushed me down on the altar of God.

* * *

The next day, I drove to the church to see Pastor Dorcas. After meeting with her, I would wait around for choir practice. I arrived five minutes late yet I spent two minutes looking at my face in the sun visor mirror. I applied some powder, darkened my purple lipstick, and brushed the thin hairs above my temples. I arranged the white pearls on my neck. I looked great. I raised the sun visor. On second thought, I brought it down again. There was nothing else to touch on my face. Pastor Dorcas had looked into my eyes the last time we saw one another. What if she liked me? I watched myself smile. What if my chi was, in fact, just helping me? I unbuttoned the top button of my shirt, tastefully and subtly exposing my cleavage. I looked perfect now.

While I waited for her secretary to announce my presence, I surfed the net on my phone, pretending that I was not jittery. My heartbeat sounded like udu drum. The secretary tapped my arm.

"I've been calling you," she said. "You may go in now."

I smiled at her and picked up my bag. I knocked on the door. I heard a very animated invitation to proceed. She sounded so close that I opened the door gently for fear of hitting her face. She was just a foot away from the door, standing by a wooden shelf, looking into a book. She grinned at me and opened her arms. I smiled and walked closer to her, almost falling on my knees to greet her. She raised me and hugged me. I sucked-in my lips to avoid staining her shoulder with my lipstick.

"Please, sit," she said, pointing to an armless upholstered chair. "I will be with you shortly."

I nodded and managed to carry myself to the chair without falling. Her perfume lingered in my nose. I had felt her nipples on my chest. They were hard. Or was it my imagination? My hands trembled. The joy in my heart was as big as tomorrow: never-ending. I tried not to get ahead of myself. I'd hugged many girls in my life, after all. But this one felt different. Anyway, all geckos lie on their stomachs so we cannot tell which one has a stomachache. I hoped that's why Pastor Dorcas had summoned me, not just to tell me about her stomachache, but to beg me to do something about it. I cautioned myself again to calm down. I moved closer to the edge of my seat and my knees brushed her orange wooden table. I felt it was a wonderful color for a table. The tabletop was white and its body orange. There was a white desktop computer on the table, white keyboards, white jotter, hell—even her pen was white. Was she trying to tell me she was pure? Had I not heard her preach against homosexuality in church? I exhaled. She did not buy that table because of me. I mean, why would she? Women and men of the cloth often preach against adultery and fornication, yet, they indulge lavishly in them. I heard her cough. I did a quick check on my cleavage to see if it was still visible. Perfect!

She sat and dragged her swivel chair closer. "Umm…Umm…" she tapped her forehead with her index finger, her pupils rolled upward.

"Forgive me I'm trying to remember your name. Oka…"

"Ọkụchi."

She snapped her finger and chuckled. "Yes, Ọkụchi. I'm sorry I forgot."

I smiled at her, my gaze on her stomach flab. I imagined resting my head on it like a soft pillow and falling asleep after a thorough love-making.

"What a unique name. What does it mean?"

"The light of God," I said.

"What a befitting name. Your voice brings light to my church, Ọkụchi," she said. "I love your purple lipstick."

I smiled. I could not look up to meet her eyes.

"On Sunday, you wore dark-green lipstick. Your weird colors of lipstick manage to do well on your chocolate skin. It's amazing."

I smiled closed-lip. My body trembled so much I could not even let her see my teeth.

"Where do you work?"

"St. Philips boys' secondary school."

"Oh, great!"

She dug out her phone from her pocket and soon the bright screen illuminated her oily face.

"Holidays are almost here. That means you will have time. The question now is would you be willing to spare your time?"

"Time for what, ma?"

She dropped her phone on the table, as though she trust me not to steal it. She picked up her white pen and relaxed in her chair. She rolled the pen in her fingers as she swiveled left to right.

"There is a music festival coming up this summer in the church I attend in the USA. The pastor asked me if I could send someone over and I accepted. After listening to you sing on Sunday, I knew I just had to send you. Let's atarodo them," she said, grinning.

She expected me to laugh when she said "atarodo" instead of "pepper," but I was shrouded in darkness. Was this why I came here? America?

"Okuchi."

I shuddered and displayed my teeth.

"You don't seem to like the idea."

"Yes, ma. I love the idea. I'm just too excited and lost for words."

Her phone rang. I thanked my lucky stars, not my chi. She picked up the phone. Soon, deep lines etched on her forehead. She pulled the phone down from her ear, covered the receiver, and whispered, "I will see you some other time."

I bobbed my head.

"Thank you for coming."

I bobbed my head.

I had not even picked up my bag when she turned her chair so her back was to me and said into the phone receiver, "Repeat what you just said."

I left. The secretary's face lit up when she saw me. I saw her lips moving, but I dashed out, not bothering to close the door behind me. I rushed to my car, flung my bag on the passenger's seat, turned my key in the ignition, and screeched out of the church parking lot. Tears burned my eyes. My chi had ridiculed me. I'd had enough. No matter how hungry a lion is, it cannot eat grass. It is who it is. I'm a lesbian. It is who I am. I can no longer hide. I stepped on the accelerator as I headed to my mother's office.

I barged into her office, panting. There were two men in blue scrubs and rubber slippers sitting on her visitor's seat. They turned to me, their eyes and mouths wide-opened enough to accommodate a cloud of flies.

"Please excuse me, gentlemen," my mother said.

They stood, closed their files, and left. My mother relaxed on her chair and folded her arms, looking at me from over her glasses. Her breathing was calm. Her eyes were peaceful. Her lips were normal. No wrinkle, no squeeze, nothing to suggest concern over why I'd barged into her office in tears. I opened my mouth. Just three words were what I planned to say: I'm a lesbian. Air flowed into my mouth. My teeth became cold and my tongue dry. I tried to talk, but I could not form the words. One jerk from my stomach pushed those three words to my throat as if my body was encouraging me to speak. But the words blocked my throat, unable to come out, unable to go back in. I felt choked. Yet, my mother sat there as calm as the moonlight.

She looked at her watch, scrunched up her lips, and folded her arms across her chest again. "You have gone to see Pastor Dorcas, haven't you?"

I nodded.

"Have you not got choir practice?"

I nodded.

"So what are you doing here, and why are you nodding like a lizard? Have you gone dumb?"

I shook my head.

She hissed. Dragging her chair closer to her desk, she opened a file. I knew it was her way of dismissing me. What she would do next was to leave me there and go. I willed myself to speak before she did that.

"Mum..."

"Look, my friend, I'm scheduled for surgery in one hour. You see those two surgeons you chased away, they are waiting for me. If you have nothing to say, go home or go to church or go get a man."

I turned, walked out, and carefully shut the door.

At home, I flung myself on my bed and cried. I'd never cried that much before. The closest to it was when I saw Austin, my friend from the university choir, lying in his coffin, his body deformed by the sickness that stilled him. I cried so much that his sister started comforting me.

This time, I cried because I did not see any way out of this, but death. I could not love a man; I could not love a woman or risk a prison term of fourteen years; I could not even have my mother's love. I flung my pillows off my bed. I picked one up, covered my face with it, and screamed. I tore off my clothes. I cried while masturbating. The orgasm felt like a joke. So I used my perfume bottle to fuck myself. I came multiple times until I was exhausted. I fell asleep.

That was how my parents found me. I heard the door open and my father's voice, "Ọkụm, are you... oh! Jesus!" The door banged shut while I scrambled for the bedsheet to wrap around my body. It was my mother's turn to charge in. She looked around, over her glasses, before her eyes settled on me. I wondered where that perfume bottle covered with my fluids was.

My mother sat on the bed. "Ọkụm, ogini?"

She called me Ọkụm. I began to cry. I wanted to hug her, but how can one hug a stone? She did not touch me, did not ask me to stop crying, did nothing. But I knew that this was the best time to tell her the truth. I imagined myself telling her how I'd fallen for Pastor Dorcas. I tell her that Pastor Dorcas is not the first elderly woman I've fallen for. Maybe I fall for older women because I am in dire need of the kind of affection my mother once had for me. She asks me to go and get married so that my husband can shower me with affection. I tell her that I cannot feel anything for any man.

"Ọkụm, what is wrong with you? What happened with Pastor Dorcas?" my mother asked again, yanking me from my head.

I shook my head. "Nothing."

"What did she want?"

"She wanted me to go to America to represent the church in something."

"And what is wrong with that?"

Words rushed to my mouth but stayed in.

"What did you expect from her, Ọkụchukwu? She is a pastor for goodness sake."

I looked at her. She pointed her twirling index finger at her temple. I guess that was what unscrewed my brain and my lips subsequently. So she knew! So she knew and she did nothing. Uchenna be damned!

"You look at everything peering over those damned glasses of yours but you do nothing. If you can see without the glasses, fling the freaking thing away!"

Her forehead furrowed. She peered at me over her glasses as though to infuriate me. She got up, adjusted her dress, and walked toward my door. She spat on the ground before gently closing the door behind her.

Mbuze

TEN-YEAR-OLD Adaugo woke under the udala tree, gasping. The voice of her mother echoed in her thoughts. She had not been sleeping well since the flood and had taken to nodding off in the shade of this tree. From where she sat, she saw a woman struggling to bathe her son as the baby played with the water. Another woman sat in front of her tent, rocking herself back and forth as she breastfed her baby. Men filled different corners of the camp, discussing. Some of them even had the effrontery to laugh. There was nothing funny. It had been two weeks since she was the girl with a father and a mother and a baby brother. One week ago, doctors and nurses in a hospital were telling her that she was an erosion survivor. And now she was alone in this camp, with others grabbed from their homes by what had come to pass between gods, nature, and men. She knew that the doctors were right. If either of her parents had survived, they would have found her by now. Yet, she held on to that hope that she was not alone. She lived in the past. The present was too painful, the future, unimaginable.

A loud belch interrupted her quiet. He was sitting on the other side of the tree, the man who belched. She could see his hairy hands, cracked heels, sand-stuffed toenails, and how his thighs spread and flattened in his faded green trousers. She wondered if the night of the flood he'd been wearing those same trousers or was he wearing, like her, the charity of the Catholic Church? She looked at the dress on her body. Whose was it before? Was the owner happy to let it go? She remembered her padlock. She touched the side of the dress and recalled that it had no side pockets. She sighed. Her eyes misted as she thought of her brother.

She remembered his small pink lips latched to one of her mother's nipples. Her mother always left her gigantic breast on the baby's mouth while she conversed with her friends. Adaugo shuddered as she recalled when her brother was just a week old and struggled to hold on to the nipple. It seemed as though that milk-filled sack held his little lips down. So Adaugo gently placed her fingers under her mother's breasts to assist her brother. Something that felt like a balloon filled with water landed on her head. She turned and saw her mother holding her breast, ready to strike again. "It's like you need a slap, ọkwia?" her mother said. She recalled when her mother, while they bathed and dressed Baby, told her that Baby's birth wiped shame from her face, made her a woman, and stamped her presence in her husband's house. Was she not stamp enough, Adaugo wondered, sitting there, beside her mother. Or would her brother turn to a stamp like the one her headmaster put on her report card?

The man in the green trousers cut short Adaugo's thoughts. "Arụ mere!" he said to another man now standing over him. "I tell you, someone committed a sacrilege against Amadioha!"

"It's not me and you that will discuss this one today. I don't have time for it," said his deep-voiced friend, as he also found a spot under the udala tree.

"I am telling you so that we can convince other men here. Let us go and find those people who see, let them help us appease Amadioha."

Adaugo wondered why diviners were always referred to as "people who see" as though the rest of them were blind.

"Appease Amadioha so that what will happen?"

"So that he will not strike us again with thunder and lightning." *Mbuze.*

Adaugo remembered that flash of lightning. She had thought the lightning looked like her father's palmar flexion, which he used to teach her psychic reading. Accompanying the lightning was a resounding thunderclap. The very ground under their feet shook. Adaugo hugged herself, covering her nose from the dust.

Her father laughed, along with his friend the headmaster, who had just arrived. "Who annoyed Amadioha?" her father asked.

"Good evening, sir," she greeted.

"Adaugo, kedụ?"

"I am fine, thank you, sir."

That was the answer she assumed he expected of her even though he spoke Igbo.

Or should I have said ọ dị mma?

She bent her head shyly. Her eyes caught her headmaster's sparkling white stockings in his brown shoes. His shirt was red polka-dotted, his tie was black, and his trousers dark green. He looked like a juicy watermelon.

"Bring our bench to our . . . you know where, Ada m."

"Yes, Nnam."

She dashed off, almost trampling on a fleeing fowl, and returned carrying the rain-softened, termite-infested wooden bench in one hand and a stronger wooden stool in the other hand. She settled the furniture on their favorite spot: under the udala tree. She ran back inside to her father's room, retrieved a bottle of Aromatic Schnapps, and two shot glasses, which she set before them.

Her father smiled and rubbed her tight newly-plaited corn-rows. "Good girl. Ngwa, sit beside me and rest."

Adaugo sat on the ground and folded her legs. That was when her mother came out, knotting her lappa tightly around her chest.

Baby must be asleep.

"I bata go?"

Can't you see him there already?

"Yes, I am back, my wife. Thank you."

She smiled at the teacher. "Onye nkuzi, nnọọ."

"Thank you. Kedụ maka obere nwa?"

"He is asleep," her mother said. "That one that wants to suck me dry."

They laughed. The second thunderclap came the moment she smiled. She had caught her father looking at her mother's onion-shaped backside absentmindedly while her mother returned to the kitchen. She smiled. Thunderclap. She felt admonished by the thunder. Her feet vibrated.

The headmaster dusted his trousers. "Let me go. This looming rain will be very heavy."

"But you only just arrived. Would you not join us for dinner?"

"If I eat your own, who will eat my wife's own? Or you think I want to come and squat in this shithole you live?"

Adaugo's father laughed, patting his friend's back. Adaugo sighted her mother approaching, carrying a tray of two covered stainless steel bowls. The headmaster stood.

"Ahn-ahn, Onye nkuzi, you can see me bringing food and you are going."

"Eeh, let me rush home before the rain starts. Next time I will settle in for a meal of nsala and mgbaduga."

Adaugo's mother tipped her head backward, closed her eyes, and laughed out loud, exposing her midline diastema and left-sided dimple. Adaugo smiled. It felt good to see her mother enjoying herself. Her mother dropped the tray on the stool, retrieved one bowl, and walked away. They bade goodbye to Onye Nkuzi.

"Come closer, Ada m, I will feed you."

Adaugo grinned and went to her father. He carried her on his lap. He uncovered the bowl and the sweet aroma of jollof rice caressed their noses. Her father pushed the rice away from the middle of the bowl, creating a hole like a volcano in the middle of the rice. Adaugo watched as steam escaped.

Mbuze.

"Jide please leave me alone," said the deep-voiced man, making it seem like the udala tree was in fact speaking. "I am not in the mood."

"I cannot leave you alone, Eze," said, Jide, raising his voice even louder as though he wanted others to hear him. "I saw it with my two eyes. Is it today that rain started falling in this town? Why then did this one kill people? Have you seen the mountain of corpses?"

Adaugo shivered. Were her parents two of the stones in that mountain?

Eze sounded angry and impatient. "I have told you that Anambra State is erosion-prone. What happened is simply erosion, mbuze. Mbuze! It has nothing to do with Amadioha. The rains have been very heavy recently and this is the peak of the rainy season. So what do you expect?"

"What I expect is for the rain to fall and go, not to cause havoc. This is no ordinary rain, Eze, I am telling you now. I saw a white ram in the sky that night. It was licking its lips as if it was drinking water. It made the lightning brighter, the rain heavier, the thunder louder. What else is a white ram if not Amadioha? If we do not do something, he will strike again, and this time, we might not survive."

Eze sighed heavily. "Were you not an illiterate, you would have heard of climate change."

"I am talking of rainy season and you are talking of climate. I don't even understand you!"

Mbuze.

It was the rainy month of July when fresh cashew and mango gave way to fresh corn and groundnut. Adaugo listened to the harmonious songs of the women, the laughter of playing children, the bleating of goats, and the *gbum-gbum-gbum* pecks between the hoe and the soil. She cradled her three-week-old brother under the orange tree while her mother combed her ridges for weeds, stopping occasionally to stretch her arms and wipe sweat from her face and neck. As dusk approached, the women and children gathered their corn, groundnuts, peppers, okra, and whatever else they'd harvested into their raffia baskets for the journey home. Adaugo frowned when her mother traded some of her beloved okra for some crazy spinach. Adaugo's mother secured Baby safely on her back using a lappa and *uja.* She balanced her basket of corn and vegetables on her head and gave the hoe to Adaugo while they joined others in the walk back to the village, via the dusty narrow road, in groups of twos and threes, children in front. Adaugo tagged along with her friend, Ngozi. Whenever a car approached, they made way, almost entering the bush. Most times, the sputtering of the crawling car or motorcycle interfered with their discussions.

"Did I tell you that . . ."

Vum-vum-vuuuuum! Pee-pee!

"Say that again?"

When they got home, Adaugo did not need to be told. First, she wiped her father's radio clean of any speck of dust. Second, she set the rubber bath and buckets for her mother to bathe Baby. She also placed the clear medium-sized plastic container, which held all Baby's clothes, on the bed. She unhooked its green lid, wondering why it had a lock hasp that was never used. After that, she picked her mud-caked blue pail from the backyard and rushed out to fetch water. Adaugo was grateful for the borehole dug by Senator Ezegbo. They no longer had to go down the two-hundred-and-fifty steps of the Ezekoro stream, carrying a pail of water on their heads. Luckily for her, the borehole was close to her house, but she missed fetching water from the stream because she no longer had an excuse to go swimming with her friends. After seven trips to the borehole, Adaugo filled their blue, plastic, water drum to the brim. She snapped the drum shut but left its padlock in the side pocket of her cream-colored dress. She made a mental note to lock it up before going to bed.

Mbuze.

"I am telling you, Jide," Eze said, "look at all the boreholes dug by that useless senator on this weak soil."

"You only wish the borehole was closer to your own house. Which other politician, apart from this one that you have tagged useless, has ever done something for this our town, Achina? Eeh?"

"All these politicians are riff-raff. Had the useless man done his assignment before drilling that bomb down the road, he would have realized that this area is very weak. His stupid borehole is what has landed us here. What has happened to us," Eze said, waving his hand at their new tent city, "will happen again and again. Achina will sink at the very thought of an earthquake."

"Then I am not afraid. Earthquake is the white man's cross," Jide said, hissing.

"You are just impossible, you this civil servant."

"And you are too unreasonable, you this akada," Jide retorted.

Adaugo wondered when "Akada" became an insult. She used to smile whenever her headmaster called her "Akada" when she excelled in class. It made her happy that an educated man called her "Academic."

"I keep telling you," Eze said, pulling himself up off the ground now. "I keep telling you all. Climate change is a reality. The world has to do something about it."

"And as I was telling you, just as with World War I and II, climate change is the white man's problem. It will not reach here."

"What kind of reasoning is that? Is it not the same earth we have?"

"We always have this discussion in my office. This earth is big. That America and Co. destroyed their air does not mean that our own air is destroyed. After all, their people die of air pollution but have you ever heard anyone here dying of air pollution?"

"What do you bunch of groundnut-eating state ministry workers know about the world?"

"Don't worry your educated head, my friend, we are safe here. Let the earth even destroy these white men, let us rule the world."

"Adaugo, they are calling you in the office."

Adaugo saw Emeka standing in front of her. She had not noticed when he came there. He looked undeterred by their refugee status. Maybe because he was with his family.

"Me?"

"Yes. They are waiting for you in the office," he said, waved at his fellow scruffy-looking friend, grinned, and ran away.

So many things crossed Adaugo's mind. Maybe Esther, the tiny woman who was in charge of feeding them, had located her parents. She was so slim that Adaugo felt she too needed the food she distributed to them. Adaugo watched her every evening as she walked around the camp, made small talk with some women, laughed, waved to others; and Adaugo wondered why she was here. Had she no family?

As Adaugo ran to the office tent after Emeka's news, she imagined her mother, sitting on a chair, breastfeeding her brother. But when she entered the room, only Esther was there. And Esther clearly read the disappointment on the girl's face.

"Adaugo, I want you to know that I have contacted your headmaster. He will come for you soon."

Onye Nkuzi is coming? Adaugo's eyes brightened. She smiled. *He is coming to take me to my parents and my brother.* She beamed. She was going home!

That night in the tent she shared with the other children still waiting for their parents, she had the recurring dream, a rearview mirror of her reality: her head heavy as if a big stone was on her neck, forcing her down, her legs immersed in water.

Her brother cries out. Her mother jumps up from the bed, clutching her chest.

"Adaugo, kedụ ihe ọ bụ?"

"Mmiri! Mmiri!"

Adaugo's mother scoops Adaugo from the floor and drops her on the bed beside her crying brother. Her father rushes in. Screams of misery everywhere.

Her mother shouts, "What is going on?"

The thunder claps louder. Strong sounds of rain on the zinc roof.

Adaugo watches her mother's hand retreat from the bed. She walks to the window, the water on the floor making *woosh-swash* sounds as her mother moves. The next lightning accompanies another thunderclap. The house shakes. Baby cries louder, waving his arms. Her mother staggers but does not fall. Adaugo watches as the water rises to her father's legs. Her mother parts the brown window curtain and looks outside, then back at her husband and children, shaking her head. She is bewildered. Another bolt of lightning. This time, it is so close that the house is illuminated for ten seconds.

"Mbuze!" her mother screams.

In a flash, that part of the house gives way with her mother in it. Adaugo deafens herself calling, "Nnem!"

Water swashes into the house and drags her father's leg. He falls but grabs one of the iron legs of the bed. Angry, hungry, the rippling water pulls at her father tearing off his lappa and exposing his manhood. The waves fling the lappa and grip the man even more forcefully. Screaming, frantic, Adaugo catches his free hand and tries to pull him up, but the water is stronger than both of them. The iron leg squeaks. Adaugo looks at her father. Shrieks of "Ewoo! Anwụola mo!" rent the air, but apart from the baby's wails, Adaugo's house is suddenly silent. Even if her father's face drips water, she sees tears fall from his eyes.

"All is well, Ada m."

Adaugo shakes her head. "No! Nnam! Please! Stay with me!"

Her father lets go of the iron leg. The water licks him up instantly. She wails, watching him struggle to stay afloat until his arms stop moving and disappear into the water. Rain pours on her, slapping her skin. Her brother shrieks. She remembers she is not alone. She turns to him. The water swallows the legs of the bed inch by inch. She turns to carry her brother, but the key in her pocket pinches her. The transparent medium-sized plastic box suddenly looks like a castle. She grabs the box and opens it. The water level grows higher to the edge of the bed. She places her brother inside the plastic box, locks it with the padlock from her pocket, and sets her brother's vessel on the water.

She watches her crying brother float away. Floating away beside him is the head of the neighbor Azuka, her body buried in the water. Her friend, Ngozi, screams as the water sweeps her away. Adaugo's house shakes again, and this time, it dissolves like salt into the roaring flood. She hears a bang as loud as thunder crashing on her head. She feels vertiginous, her head heavy again. Everywhere becomes black, but the cries of woe still drum in her ears as her body surrenders to the unrelenting current.

The roar of water fills her ears; the words of others fill her thoughts.

That one that wants to suck me dry.

All is well, Ada m.

A man who fears a lot dies so many times.

Mbuze.

Croscat Volcano

CRISTINA WALKED DOWN the sloppy mountain leading to the Croscat volcano. She'd been a healthy pharmacist until five days ago when she developed severe chest pain and shortness of breath. Now, she was a metastatic breast cancer patient. Well, not just cancer, that would have been somewhat hopeful, but the wicked thing had gone unnoticed and had eaten deep into her lungs. Cristina knew she was a dead woman already. She smiled as she remembered the face of the worried Swedish doctor who vainly attempted to start her on immediate treatment. Cristina insisted that there was no need. Though she was only thirty-seven, she believed that she was done here.

She stopped suddenly and palmed her chest as if she could soothe the sharp pain as a beloved crying baby. Love, they say, can thaw a frozen heart. But can love thaw cancer? She stood there for a few minutes to catch her breath. She was surrounded by greenness save for the narrow sandy path. After five deep breaths—she made sure she counted—she gulped from her water bottle and continued counting her steps. She narrowly avoided stepping on the tail of a baby snake wandering off the trail.

Cristina had been afraid of so many things in her life: like this, going to the volcano, through the forest, unaccompanied. Swimming used to be on the list, but she had defeated that only yesterday. Next, she would defeat her fear of heights by going skydiving or taking a ride in a hot air balloon. Knowing she would soon be dead, fear was needless.

She was also gamophobic. Her parents' marriage was terrible. Marriage scared Cristina. But she was in love with Eduardo. It had been twenty-two good years of love. Eduardo was willing to remain her partner even if he would have preferred the title "husband." Though Cristina was afraid of being a selfish parent, like her Igbo mother and Catalan father, she wished to carry Eduardo's babies, and he so very badly wanted her to carry them as well. But because of Cristina's parents' toxic marriage, Eduardo suffered. Even when she left him, once, out of guilt, he searched for her, he found her, and he loved her.

Now, she was ready to have children. She was ready to take the chance. She was ready to stop being selfish and make Eduardo happy. For five years, she had sought a child. She could not take in naturally. But in vitro fertilization did the magic, though paying for it milked her bank account dry, and Eduardo's too. She was three months pregnant; she had cancer, and she was going to die.

She pulled her thick, coarse black hair to see if it would come off. It did not. She felt another sharp pain in her chest. She stopped again. She felt very tired. Her heart wouldn't stop beating fast. Was it just the symptoms or was it the fear of death? She needed to conquer fear before she died. That's why she'd insisted on leaving busy Barcelona for the serenity of Olot. That was why she chose to stay in Hotel Riu Fluvia. She needed the cake of the quietness the hotel provided, and the icing of the genuine smiles on the faces of the staff. But nothing could be compared to looking out from her balcony and watching the beauty of the green mountains and the white clouds. The hot air balloons, they made her mornings. It felt as if she was staring at the cover of a romance novel.

Cristina arrived at the foot of the volcano. She looked up at the high sandy rock and sighed. Hadn't the cab driver told her that Croscat was the youngest and tallest volcano in Catalonia? It was so amazing that she could not wait to get to her next stop, Volcano Santa Margarida. Why have I been so afraid? Nature is beautiful, she thought.

"I am surprised that you are still alive," the doctor had replied when she asked how much time she had to live.

Those words would not stop haunting her.

She smiled.

She chuckled.

She laughed.

She had already cheated death.

She laughed again.

Yes, she'd cheated death! She laughed so loud. It felt good to laugh again. She hadn't enjoyed a good laugh in five days. She laughed louder, felt it through her entire being, felt it underneath her feet.

She stopped laughing, but the earth kept shaking. She looked around and saw tree branches shivering like someone with a fever. She broke out in a sweat. Everywhere smelled like burning sand. Should she run? To where? It's not as if she could outrun nature. She shook her head in resignation and looked up to the sky, where she would probably spend the night, and eternity. The earth shook again.

"I love you, Eduardo," she whispered. "May you find love."

The earth's movement became even more vehement. Cristina stood there prepared. The words of the doctor kept ringing in her head: *I am surprised that you are still alive.* Death found her alive—that is all that matters.

"Nature is beautiful indeed," she whispered right before the sand sliding speedily down the mountain buried her.

All Shades Of Senselessness

SOMKENE SIPPED FROM her glass of nonalcoholic wine, changing the TV channels for want of something to do, yet Ebube would not stop whining.

"And to think that I had to stand all day, yesterday, working for that mumu bank. The banking hall was filled to the brim as if someone blew a whistle announcing that if you did not transact with the bank you will die. Now, what do I get early this morning? Termination letter!"

Somkene yawned. "Ebube, it is okay. Die it."

"Die it, keep calm, how easy for you to say. How can I keep calm as if everything is okay? I just lost my job!"

"You never liked it anyway. You should be happy. We should be celebrating. You need a refill."

Somkene filled Ebube's glass.

Ebube shook her head. "Celebrate? After three years of slaving for that madhouse bank, they toss me out like a piece of rubbish. How, in God's name, will I afford to pay my rent?"

Somkene chuckled, sipped her wine, and placed her glass on the glass side stool, dreading the sound it made when the two met. She picked up her phone. She heard Ebube murmur something and hiss, but she did not quite get what it was Ebube said. Somekene felt sorry for her friend. Even if Ebube would not admit it, Somkene knew that her greatest fear was returning to Enugu to burden her parents.

"Your rent is how much, again?"

Ebube turned to her, looking confused.

Somekene focused on her phone. "The rent you are whining about is how much?"

"Four hundred k."

Somekene stopped pressing her phone and looked at her. "That is a lot."

Ebube pulled her hair. "Why do you think I want to run mad on account of losing this job?"

"You will get another one, surely, but don't you think you should move to a cheaper flat so that you can save yourself some money? Better still, move in here. How many times do I have to offer you a room here?"

"My sister, I cannot stay in this house, please. Forget that one."

"You're bloody well working for your landlord! You work and send him the entire money!"

"Somkene, why are you exaggerating?"

Somekene resumed pressing her phone. "Ọ bụ asị?"

Ebube sighed. She set her wine glass on the table and her head on the headrest. A beep from her phone startled her. She picked up the phone, complaining that she did not want to attend to sympathizers, but what she saw made her sit up immediately, wipe her eyes, and peer at her phone. She looked at Somkene, eyes wide, and back to her phone. She wiped her palm on her skirt, wiped her eyes, smearing her mascara, and gazed back at the phone, holding it very close to her face in case she had just developed myopia. She wiped the phone on her chest, and, this time, used her fingers to place imaginary commas on her screen.

It still amounted to one million naira. It did not seem possible that a Nigerian, especially in the looming recession, would give another Nigerian one million naira just like that—even if their father was Dangote.

"Ọgịnị?" Somkene asked.

Ebube looked at her. She looked back at the phone, then back at Somkene. Her mouth was open but no words were uttered.

"Yes, I sent you a million naira. So what?"

Ebube gazed at Somkene.

"Use the money to pay your rent for two years. Survive on the change until you find something else to do. I always admire people like you who work hard to survive. I have never had to work in my life, let alone work a job that I hate."

Black tears rolled down Ebube's cheeks. "Thank you so much, Somkene."

"What are friends for? Just, please, stop complaining. The job is gone. It is gone. Move on."

Just then the intercom beside Somekene rang. She answered, said "Yes?" and returned the handset to the cradle.

"My mother wants me. Wait for me. I shall be back soon."

"No." Ebube drank up her wine. "Let me go home. We go see."

Somkene chuckled.

"No comment. Let me go and answer my mother, abeg."

They shared a hug. Ebube left.

Somkene found her mother upstairs seated on her king-sized bed, head bent, fingers looped. There was a big brown envelope beside her. When Somkene called her, she looked up and managed a starved smile.

"Are you all right?" Somkene asked.

"Sure." Her mother patted the bed. "Sit, nwam."

Somkene obeyed. Her mother picked up the brown envelope and handed it to her.

"Take this document to your father in his hotel room."
Somkene collected the envelope. "Did he annoy you again?"
Her mother smiled weakly. "I am fine. Don't worry. Just go
and deliver this to him, please. He needs it urgently."

"All right. I will get to it immediately."

"You have to drive yourself. I sent your driver on an errand
and he is not back yet."

"No problem, Mummy."

She squeezed Somkene's hand very tightly and held on to
her for a while. She sighed. "Please go with your phone too in
case I need to reach you."

Somkene smiled. "Isn't that why they are called mobile
phones?"

Somkene walked the long corridor to her room wondering what her parents must have fought about this time. They
were always at odds. She felt her mother's weakness when
she squeezed her palm. Whatever fight her mother had with
her father must have reached into her chest and punched her
heart. She felt sorry for her mother, who was a perfect example
of the saying, "money cannot buy happiness." Her father was
an unapologetic philanderer. The disgust for his huge sexual
appetite was directly responsible for Somekene's decision to
remain a virgin. She entered her room, picked out a straight
blue dress and changed, brushed her wavy weave, and was out
of the house.

* * *

Third Mainland Bridge was free of gridlock. Somkene was
delighted. She recalled when she first came back to Lagos from
the UK, much to her chagrin because her father wanted her to
understudy him in preparation to become the new CEO of his

company, which assembled cars. The infamous Lagos traffic taught her a lesson when she spent two hours going from Alausa to Otedola estate, a journey that should not exceed five minutes. She could not believe how much of her precious time got roasted sitting in the car. She asked her father for a driver as soon as she got home. The new driver started the very next morning. She smiled. No matter how disrespectful her father had been to her mother, she loved him. He denied her nothing: but one request. When she was informed that she was to take over her father's company, even though she was the last of seven sisters, she declined and begged her father to give it to any of her siblings. He insisted that the job was hers. Hence, she had to quit her beloved... the sound of her ringing phone jarred her. It was her mother.

"Nne, how far have you gone?"

"I have just crossed Third Mainland Bridge. I will soon be in Adeola Odeku. Ọginị?"

"Ọnwerọ. Nothing."

"You want me to come back?"

"It is okay. Go."

Somkene knew her mother must have called to say something she did not say.

She arrived at her father's five-star hotel. He called it *Fabine*, which was coined from Fabian, his name, and "ne" from her "Somkene." As she pulled up, her phone rang again.

"Where are you?"

"I have just gotten to the hotel."

"That was fast. I should not have asked you to drive yourself."

She hung up. Somkene wondered what it was that her mother could not bring herself to say. She smiled and waved at the receptionists when they called out their greetings. She knew her father's room. His staff members were always lodged in his hotel for training and meetings, and he would lodge with them. Everyone knew why he did that, but no one dared raise an eyebrow.

The lift opened to the fifth floor. The rooms on that floor were soundproofed to give the guests who could afford those rooms some privacy to go mad. She sighted his suited bodyguards standing outside his door at the far end of the corridor. She smiled at them as she approached. They returned her courtesy and opened the door. She entered the red suite. It smelled of cigarettes. Two of her father's guards stood there like statues. She found her father sitting on his bed in the room, smoking. He wore a white singlet and a white laced trouser. He tapped the spot beside him. She sat there, dropping the envelope in his outstretched hand.

"I've been expecting you," he said. His breath smelled of wine and tobacco.

"Sorry. I came as fast as I can."

He opened the envelope and scanned through the documents. "Ejike, pour her a drink," he said, not looking up from his papers.

"No need, Ejike. I don't need a drink."

Ejike went back to stand like a statue. Somkene and her father got talking about business. They discussed at length while he smoked and sipped his wine. Somkene was uncomfortable with the number of cigarettes he smoked per day, but the real discomfort came when he placed a hand on her lap. She stiffened, but it was her father. She reprimanded herself for even thinking that he had ulterior motives. He slid his hands further up her thighs.

She hit his hand away. "Dad, kedụ ịfeọbụ? Ọdịkwa na mma?"

Could he no longer tell the difference between his daughter and his numerous girlfriends?

He smiled slyly and placed his hand where it was before. Somkene knocked it off and stood to leave, convinced her father was drunk. But the guards blocked her way. She looked at her father, expecting him to order them to get out of the way, but he did no such thing. Instead, he commanded her to sit. Somkene's palms became sweaty. Her father got up to refill his glass.

"Let me enlighten you a little on some secret cultures we have in Igboland," he said.

Somekene thought of what to do. How would she escape the two guards inside and the two others outside? She looked around for a potential weapon, not that it would do her any good.

"It is no longer news that girls cannot inherit lands in Igboland," he said.

Somkene shifted uneasily.

"So, when a rich man who isn't polygamous has only female children, there will be a need for a male child who would inherit his lands in the village. What the family does is to pick one of the daughters who would not be allowed to get married. Instead, she would stay at home and give birth to a boy who would bear her father's name. Only when she bears a son is she free to marry. In my case, since I don't want to remarry, because I am not polygamous, and I don't want to cloth your mother with shame, and considering that your mother can no longer bear children, both of us have settled this."

Somkene felt her head expand.

"Your mother and I have decided that you are the one who would stay at home to bear us a male child."

Even though the AC was chilling, Somkene felt like a melting snowman.

"Now, because of my social and political standing, and because I will hate for a nonentity to come claiming my son, I have decided to be the one to impregnate you."

"What!" she shouted. "What!"

"Yes?"

"You want to sleep with your own child! Do you even know what incest means?"

He guffawed. He pointed at his guard and pointed at Somkene. "She is talking about incest."

The statues remained unmoving.

"Please get me a Bible," he said, still laughing.

Ejike hastily went to the sitting room and returned, bowing as he handed his boss a Bible.

"Open it, open it," Somkene's father said, waving his hands dismissively. "Read Genesis chapter nineteen verse thirty-two."

The sound of shuffling pages filled Somkene's ears.

"Come, let us make our father drink wine, and we will lie with him, that we may preserve the lineage of our father," read Ejike.

"Thank you." Somkene's father sipped his wine.

Ejike made to close the book but Somkene's father held up his hand. "Hold on with that, Ejike. We still have one more passage to study."

Turning to Somkene, he said, "Why did the daughters lie with their father, Lot?"

He did not wait for a response.

"Because they want to preserve the lineage of their father. Would you call that incest? Is it not the same preservation of lineage that I seek?"

He refilled his wine glass. "Read from the same Genesis, chapter twenty, verse twelve."

He sipped his wine, looking up, while the guard read out loud again.

"But indeed, she is truly my sister. She is the daughter of my father, but not the daughter of my mother, and she became my wife."

"Thank you, Ejike. You may drop the Bible now."

He smiled at Somkene.

"That was Abraham speaking. He said his wife, Sarah, is his sister. Is that incest or not? Was it permitted by God or not? Did it stop God from blessing Abraham or not?"

He put down his glass and moved closer to Somkene, squatted before her, and held her hands. She pulled her hands away.

He whispered, "I have taken my time to explain to you that God will not frown at us for having sex. So, why don't we just have fun? Just relax." He kissed her lap.

She pushed him forcefully, and he toppled over, sounding like a hardcover book crashing on tiles.

"Dad, please, don't do this to me. Please. If you let me leave, I will pretend this discussion never happened."

He laughed and stood. Somkene climbed onto the bed for want of where to go.

"Do not stress me, Somkenechukwu."

He pointed at her, mounting the bed. Somkene scurried away before he could grab her.

He commanded his guards. "Bring that idiot here, fools!"

They caught Somkene and pinned her to the bed. Her ear-slicing scream rent the air. But seeing the calm and unperturbed looks on their faces, she remembered that the room was soundproofed. Confused, she begged her father again.

"Biko, Nnam, biko. I am a virgin. Please!"

He grinned. As she begged, Ejike pushed her dress up while the other guard held her hands. She struggled, screaming her head off. She saw her naked father—she had no idea when he'd removed his clothes—climb on top of the bed and tear her panties away with one hand like a hungry predator. She kept screaming and struggling. She felt his hand rub her sex. Then she felt him part her labia with his index and middle fingers.

"Get me my shower gel!" he barked at the guard who was holding Somkene's hands.

Once the guard left her hands, she started raining beatings on her father. He bent his head to shield his face. She tore at his neck and drew blood.

"Ejike, onye nzuzu!" he screamed. "Hold her hands, will you?"

Ejike obeyed swiftly. The first blow landed on her cheek. Somkene closed her eyes as the pain shot through her body. Another blow landed on her left eye. She screamed, but she was too pressed down into the bed to even shake. She tried to open her eyes, but it felt very heavy and painful. Nonetheless, she was able to see her father's fat fist coming for her. She shut her eyes tight and turned her face away, exposing her left ear to the incoming fist. She started hearing songs, in fortissimo, in her left ear as if a choir of mosquitoes had gathered there. She tried to make out the lyrics of the mosquito song when she felt something cold and slimy between her legs. She knew it was the shower gel. She felt her father's fingers rub it. Her eardrums were preoccupied with "drumming for the mosquito choir" that she did not hear when he barked an order for another ointment. She felt something watery drop on her. Her left eye felt as if someone poured pepper in it.

Somkene screamed until she felt she had lost her voice. She was afraid her father's penis, which was busy down there, would travel up her body and show up in her tonsils. She vomited. Her thighs were held so far apart that she thought her tendons would tear. Her body was in so much pain. She began to imagine if this was what childbirth felt like. But her mind, which was the only active thing in her, reminded her she was not giving birth. *So, if sex was this painful, why then do people rush for it?* Her mind responded that she was being raped. Raped! Raped by her father. Somkene wanted to die. Up till now, she had not been able to understand why people committed suicide. Why on earth would someone just want to die? But now, she wanted to die. Maybe the pain would kill her. Maybe if she stopped strug-gling, death would take over. The *mosquito choir in her ears* sang in diminuendo when she heard her father moaning loudly. She wished she could take over from the mosquito's conductor and take them back to fortissimo.

She was still lying there like a corpse when the weight on her body deserted her. She felt hollowed out. Her thighs and hands were free and not pinned. But the pains in her eyes, ears, and hips were still there. She tried to lift her hand, but she could not. She tried to open her eyes, lift a finger, a toe, shake anything, but her body did not obey her. It occurred to her that she might be dead. She heard when her father gave his thugs instructions to carry her down the back stairs, into the car, and then drive her home. So, if she was dead, how come she could hear? Did they not say that hearing was the last sense to die during death? Maybe she was indeed dead. She tried to move again, but she could not. She knew, however, when she was lifted. She knew when her hands and her head dangled because it felt as if all the blood in her body had collected in her head. She knew when she was dropped on a surface. She heard the sound of the car. She knew when she was dangling again. Then she heard a wail.

"What happened to her? What have you people done to her?"

It sounded like her mother's voice. She felt safe. She knew when she touched another surface. She heard her mother's voice shout, "Get out!" She tried to smile victoriously, but she could not smile.

* * *

Somkene opened her eyes. First, they felt sore and painful. Her left eye felt loaded as if a bucket of stones sat on it. She could open only her right eye. Everywhere was white. Was she in heaven? Then her vision became blurry. She blinked to see clearer. She saw her mother. The woman was crying and smiling. She tried to move her body to be sure that she could move it now, but her mother pressed her down.

"Lie down. The doctor said you must rest. Thank God you are awake."

She tried to speak, but her lips were sore.

"You have been unconscious for three days," her mother offered.

Somkene was shocked to hear that. Three days! She felt a sudden twinge on her right hand. She opened her right eye and saw her mother still smiling. There was another woman in the room holding her hand. Memories of Ejike and his fellow criminals holding her hands flooded her head. She started struggling, but her mother helped the woman to hold her still.

"It is okay. The nurse just wants to inject you," her mother said, softly.

Somkene relaxed. When they were done with the injection, she felt sleepy.

"Don't worry, nnem, you will soon be fine."

It took two more days for her to be able to eat and talk. Her left eye was still plastered, but the pain had reduced. Her mother was there, as usual. Somkene was impatient to tell her mother what her father did to her. She spoke so fast. She believed that her father lied when he said his wife was in the know. Her mother lowered her head and listened quietly and motionlessly. Her mother did not appear surprised by the news. Somkene then assumed that her father must have confessed. So, why had he not checked on her? Had he been arrested? She sighed. Her mother would never have the nerve to arrest her "god" of a husband.

"Daddy has confessed, hasn't he?"

Her mother raised her head. Somkene did not know the woman was crying.

"I'm sorry, Somkene." She held her daughter's hand. "I did not know it will be this brutal."

"What," Somkene whispered.

The dots started adding up and making sense.

"Your father forced me to agree to it or he would throw us out and remarry. I have no bank account of my own. If he throws us out, where would I go? How would I bear the shame? I had to agree. Besides, it is our tradition."

She sniffled and blew her nose. "It is the life of a woman. Women are properties, tools for childbearing . . ."

Somkene stopped listening. She had been betrayed by her family. Why did she wake up? A peaceful death would have been better. She felt her mother touch her.

"Please, my child, accept what has happened. Let us pray that you will bear a son so that there won't be a repeat of this."

"I want to be alone. Please just go away."

* * *

During the next two days, Somkene's physical recovery was swift, but her mind drowned further into depression. Her life had been planned for that rape. Her life had been all shades of senselessness, but she had been deliberately blinded by flattery and luxury. No wonder when, at age twenty-two, she brought her suitor to her father, he told her she was too young for marriage. Meanwhile, her eldest sister got married at twenty-one. No wonder her mother had recently been interested in her menstrual cycle, asking her when she would start bleeding and when she would stop. She touched her stomach. What if she was already pregnant? Pregnant for her father? She shook her head. She would abort the baby. What if she died doing that? She did not want to die that way. Would she bear the child, assuming she was pregnant, and give the child up for adoption? Would she abscond? What if she was not pregnant? No. Death was the best way out. She would take an overdose of her drugs, die, and rest. Option two. She would have to start by leaving the house, leaving the luxury she was accustomed to, leaving all the money behind. She would go to Ebube's house. From there, she would think up what next to do. Yes!

No.

Yes?

Maybe.

Acknowledgments

My dad started reading my stories when I was only a child. Each time, he would pat my head and say, "Well done, you are trying." One day, I replied, "No, I am not trying, I've gotten there." I remember he enjoyed a burst of hearty laughter: alone. It would take almost three decades for my words to become reality. Filled with eternal gratitude, I have been looking at this page, unable to craft feelings into words. My journey is not mine alone. It's a story filled with characters and scenes of joy and laughter and tears.

Chukwu okike, the creator, protector, the almighty, I would not be writing this without your blessings. I owe you all that I am and will ever be. You are faithful and merciful and loving and kind. May your spirit hover around, guiding and guarding the following heroes:

My beloved parents, *ndị ọ ga-adịlị mma*, Chief Dominic Ezeamama (Ojekanwehi Ezenwadiebube 1 of Achina) and Mrs. Gloria Ezeamama (Ada Achina tiri ego na bank). My eyes mist just thinking of how to thank you for all you have done and been to us: my siblings and me. *Chukwu dobe unu.*

Kaima and Zikora. Love made sense when you showed up. My love for you is larger than the animal that swallowed a blue whale whole. Your love is the cloak I wear. It is the reason I get up every night and write.

My siblings, my strength, my support, *ike m kwo aba, echeta obi esie ike, ndị ọma.* Adaobi Ezeamama, Chigozie Ezeamama, Ogechi Ezeamama, Ifeoma Ezeamama, Chinonye Ezeamama, Oluchi Ezeamama, Chinonso Okafor Ima-imande, and my beloved tomorrow, Chimeremeze Ezeamama (my nephew). I pray, amongst other things, that all of your dreams come true.

To my editor at Sandorf Passage, Buzz Poole, *nwoke ọma,* thank you for being very thorough with my work. Your understanding of my stories, despite not being an Igbo man, is as pure and as gentle as a dove. You are the best editor anyone could ask for.

Frances Ogamba, a sister from another mother, *enyi m ji eje mba, ezigbo enyim,* my first reader who is always sincere enough to say, "What are you writing? Biko jebezie na anyị anụgo."

Ebere Loretta James, Beluchi Ezeliora Emedosi, Blessing Chibuzo Obidikẹ, Sambasa Nzeribe, Ifeachukwu Orjiani, Fr. Jude Nwachukwu, Irene Garcia Losquino, Maddie Kurchik, Nina Carlsson, Charo Reyes, Declan Taggart, and all those who do not want their names to be called: God bless you.

While querying agents and publishers for this book, rejections attacked like *mbuze.* But of all the shades of "unfortunately" I had to deal with, there was not a single response of "nobody knows where Nigeria is." For this, my eternal gratitude goes to all the amazing Nigerian writers, bathed in beauty and grace and determination, those lovelies who put our country on the literary map. They gave us a voice. They pushed through closed doors and held them open for us. *Ndi odogwu! Ebube dike! Igodo ọla edo! Aka m di n'elu.* Thank you.

KASIMMA

To those listed here and to those I cannot mention for want of space, thank you. *Daalu riine.*

Ọnụ m juru na-ekene.

About Sandorf Passage

SANDORF PASSAGE publishes work that creates a prismatic perspective on what it means to live in a globalized world. It is a home to writing inspired by both conflict zones and the dangers of complacency. All Sandorf Passage titles share in common how the biggest and most important ideas are best explored in the most personal and intimate of spaces.